Out of Love

C. Fleming Johnson

authorHOUSE®

AuthorHouse™
1663 Liberty Drive
Bloomington, IN 47403
www.authorhouse.com
Phone: 1-800-839-8640

First published by AuthorHouse   10/1/2009

ISBN: 978-1-4389-7202-2 (sc)
ISBN: 978-1-4389-7203-9 (hc)

Printed in the United States of America
Bloomington, Indiana

This book is printed on acid-free paper.

Cover Artist:
Monica Linares
Apex, North Carolina

TO:

The 9 year old who never gave up her dream!

Chapter One

Standing motionless in front of a well-stocked closet of designer clothes as though glued in place, Cynthia Farrell shakes her head as if annoyed with what she is seeing. "Why is it always so hard lately to pack for a trip? You would think after all these years I would be able to do this with my eyes closed." Realizing how she sounds her inner voice kicks in, *C'mon girl, get over it, get the stuff, throw it in the suitcase and get on with it.* Shaking her head and smiling she reaches for two suits, one black, one gray and a just in case gorgeous and very sexy little black dress to complete what she has already laid across the bed to pack. As she lifts the sexy little black dress from its special place in her closet, she couldn't help but chuckle. Holding it up in front of her she thinks, *you know I never thought of myself as the sexy black dress type but I'm glad Joyce talked me into buying* this *one,* recalling the day several months ago when she and best friend Joyce Carver were in Nordstrom's at Short Hills Mall, "get it, get it" Joyce screams. "That dress has your name written all over it."

"Joyce have you lost your mind, I could never wear anything like this – it, it just shows too much."

"Oh come on," snaps Joyce. "You can't tell anything by just standing there holding it. Try it on. Besides, why are you working out at the gym almost every day? You look super fine for a woman of any age – flaunt it girl."

Swinging around to the full length mirror near her closet, she stares longingly at her image. "You know sexy black dress, Joyce was right – I do look good for my age. Good heavens! I can't believe I just said that - how vain!" A smile comes over her face thinking about the final meeting held in Gaftgo's boardroom and the dinner that followed that night at The Four Seasons in Manhattan, when she wore the dress. "Hmm, I wonder if the dress had anything to do with sealing the deal for me on the Gaftgo/Pharmil merger? Shaking her head, as she continues to stare at herself in the mirror with the dress tucked under her chin, "nah," she says, "it was a done deal before they got a look at me in this dress."

Her presentation was flawless, Fred Hoban, Gaftgo's CEO even stood up and applauded when she finished. "Brilliant Cynthia, simply brilliant," he bellowed. "We are all going into New York for dinner at The Four Seasons, you are planning to join us, right?" She started to say no, but knew just what consequences saying no might have. She truly disliked these after meeting get togethers, but her boss was a stickler for them. He honestly believed the real deals were cemented outside the boardroom. "I wouldn't miss it for anything," trying to sound like she really meant it. "Look forward to seeing you later Cynthia," calls Fred as he and his staff leave the boardroom.

As the room clears there sits Jason Benedict at the other end of the table, grinning from ear to ear with that 'I told you so look on his face.'

"Okay boss, don't even think about saying a word. Just let me pack up my stuff and I will meet you later."

"Cynthia" he chides, "how could you even think I would say anything other than echoing Fred's words – brilliant, just brilliant."

"Thank you, now leave."

"Anything you say, oh brilliant one. I just wanted to let you know that I hired a car to take us to The Four Seasons. It will swing by here to get me and then we'll stop by your house."

"Okay," says Cynthia matter-of-factly. "I'll be – no wait, I almost forgot. I'm staying at the company suite tonight. I thought I told you that a couple of weeks ago?"

"You probably did. But, no problem, I'll swing by the company suite to get you around 5:30. We are scheduled to meet Fred and the crew for drinks at Chez Josephine on 42nd Street around 6:30 before dinner. Great job Cyn, really a great job. I am very proud of you."

"You know Jason, I am very proud of myself right now."

"Well you should be you put everything you had into this project so you deserve to sit back and take pleasure in how it turned out. This was a major coup for both of us. Enjoy it then go and make yourself lovelier than usual, I think Chairman Hoban would like that."

"Will you just get out of here, please! I am not the one for sale."

Turning from her closet and walking toward the still unpacked suitcase, "but I sure felt like I was that night" she says out loud. Holding the dress up in front of her she swings around and walks toward the full length mirror. Pressing the dress to her well-shaped body she smiles as she remembers the expression on Jason's face as he stepped out of the limo to greet her, but never said a word about her dress or the way she looked that night. But the expression on his face spoke volumes. Starting to laugh, "I could never tell if he was impressed or just thought I had lost my mind."

For Cynthia that night was no different than any other time this group got together for dinner after a meeting. But it was the first time she had ever worn a dress of this type - clinging in the most appropriate places, cut low enough to reveal a very desirable bust line and short enough to reveal the shapely legs of someone who spent over 20 years in dance class. This look was very different for her - light years away from her standard 'it's all about business suits' and Ferragamo shoes. That night the shoes were the black silk Manolo Blahnik pumps with 5 inch heels Joyce convinced her to buy and which took three weeks to learn how to walk in.

She really liked the way she looked and it showed as she stepped from the limo and entered Chez Josephine totally oblivious to being the center of attention until Fred Hoban spotted her. As he walked toward her she couldn't help but notice his eyes never fixed on her face but were aimed directly at the low-cut neckline. As she remembers the expression on his face, she lets out a howl.

"Cynthia, what the heck are you doing out there?" calls Arthur from the bathroom, startling her out of her strange mood.

"I'm packing Arthur," still staring at the little black dress and laughing. "What the heck are you doing in there? You've been in there for almost an hour."

"Well, I have a tough day coming up. I'm meeting with the Mayor and the Governor and there is a press conference scheduled right after the meeting so I want to make sure I get my look just right," Arthur shouts back.

"Don't we all," she says with a smile and still holding on to her little black dress.

"Hey Cyn – how long do you think you will be in New Orleans," calls Arthur from the bathroom.

She smiles as she thinks of the man she has been married to for 37 years – who always needs something when she is on the phone or only seems to be interested in carrying on a conversation when he is in the bathroom. Some things never change and Arthur is definitely one of those things.

"Cyn, did you hear me?" shouts Arthur, "how long?"

"I heard you Art. We went over my schedule last night. Why is it you can never remember from one minute to the next what I've said?"

"What did you say – how long?" Arthur shouts again.

Turning away from the bed and crossing the room toward the closed bathroom door, she places her forehead on the door. "Art," she says slowly and deliberately, "how many times have I told you to wait until we are in the same room to ask me a question. You always look for information when you know that unless you're standing right next to me you are not going to hear what I have to say."

"I can hear you Cyn, I'm not deaf."

"I know you are not deaf my darling, but you don't pay attention."

"So how long are you going to be in New Orleans?"

Shaking her head and heading back toward the bed to finish packing, she realizes that she cannot win. Arthur is exactly the same today as he was 43 years ago when they first met. "Probably two weeks," she calls out.

"Two weeks! You're kidding, right? Why so long Cyn?"

"Arthur Farrell I am not going to continue to have a conversation through a closed bathroom door."

"Okay, okay," as he emerges from the bathroom slowly making his way toward her in the same manner he did when they first met. "When I get the Arthur Farrell full name and voice, I know when to stop."

Cynthia starts laughing, "Well, it is nice to know that you have learned something about me after all these years."

"That's not fair Cyn you know I can't do anything without you. It just isn't the same without you around here," now purring with his 'little boy done wrong face on'. "You're my rock Cynthia and I am really lost without you. I miss you an awful lot when you are not around me."

"Oh please," she laughs. "When I'm dead and buried, you will do just fine without me around. Besides, if you keep looking this good there will be a lot of women standing in line outside this front door ready to make sure you won't even remember my name."

As he moves closer with arms outstretched she sees before her - six feet, four inches of fashion elegance draped in a well-tailored dark gray pinstriped suit with coordinating shirt and tie, with barely a wrinkle to show for his 63 years and not more than 10 pounds over the 190 he weighed the day they married. The few sprinkles of grey at his temples and in his well-clipped moustache add to the charm and elegance of this man she has known for more than half her life and, of course, the shoes – black this time not mocha. Through all the years and fashion trends he has stayed true to his Johnston & Murphy cap-toe shoes. Even when casually dressed, no Gucci loafers for this guy.

"Hey, don't say things like that. You know you will outlive me."

"Arthur, you have been using that phrase for as many years as I have known you. I'm starting to think you really believe that."

Dropping his arms, "okay I know where this is going, forget it. Now, why two weeks and do you really think I look that good?"

Chapter Two

Arthur Farrell was 20 when 15 year old Cynthia met him. Her best friend Joyce Carver called to tell her about this gorgeous guy she just met, who was a senior at the Wharton School in Pennsylvania and visiting his Mom who just moved to Montclair from Topeka, Kansas so she could be near him when he started Rutgers Law School. He didn't know anyone in the neighborhood and to come over to meet him. Joyce thought every guy she just met was gorgeous, so she almost didn't go. Joyce at 17 spent most of her time thinking and talking about boys and complaining that Cynthia always had her head stuck in a book.

When she walked into Joyce's living room Arthur was already there. As she moved toward them, Arthur stood up and slowly walked toward her with his arm outstretched to shake her hand. In a quick second her eyes went from the top of his neatly cut hair, to his deep caramel colored skin, to his well-tailored tan slacks and coordinating shirt, tie and sweater, then to his feet. For the longest she let her eyes linger on his shoes – mocha colored Johnston & Murphy cap-toe shoes, thinking 'holy cow this is definitely not the fashion of the day, only my Dad and a couple of his friends dress like they descended from royalty.'

Cynthia loved the fact that her Dad was well-known in the community for his style and way of dressing. Every day, rain or shine, Cecil Tate looked as though he just stepped out of the pages of a fashion magazine with his Homburg hat, expertly tailored dark blue or gray suit, exquisite tie and shirt and wing-tipped shoes. For as long as she could remember, Cynthia never saw her father in anything other than a dark blue suit for dress, a gray suit for those casual times, and the obligatory black suit for funerals and other somber occasions. He always looked as though he was on his way to meet the Queen of England - definitely not at all the dress of a typical working man. When he worked in the yard he had on shoes, trousers with suspenders and a shirt with the sleeves neatly rolled up to his elbows. The only thing missing: his tie and Homburg hat. Without them, this was his version of casual dress.

Now moving toward her was this very handsome young man who reminded her of her father. *Good heavens, she thinks, who does he think he is and what kind of a boy dresses like this in 1965! Hasn't he ever heard about sneakers or sandals, jeans and dashikis or tie-dyed tee shirts and foot high afros?* Her eyes were so fixed on his shoes she never heard him introduce himself or saw his extended hand.

"Cynthia, Cynthia," shouts Joyce. "Are you in there?"

Jolted by the sound of Joyce's voice, "What, what! Oh, I'm sorry. How do you do," she says as she reaches to accept his outstretched hand, "I'm Cynthia Tate."

"He knows that already Cyn," says an annoyed Joyce "you zoned out for a while." Turning to look at Arthur, "forgive her Arthur, she isn't always this scatter-brained she's really very smart."

"Okay Joyce I get your point," says an equally annoyed Cynthia. But from that point on it didn't take long for her to realize he was very, very different from all the other boys she had ever met. His English was perfect, the way he pronounced certain words you could hear every syllable, every word ending. How easy he switched from one topic to another, making everything sound as though she was hearing it for the first time. Every time she looked at him, she knew he would be in her life. When her hand gently touched his out-stretched hand - she knew. When she raised her eyes from his mocha colored Johnston & Murphy shoes and looked into his - she knew they would be together always.

For years, that was the joke in their house – Arthur loved to tell everyone about their first meeting "would you believe she fell in love with my shoes before she even looked at me and since she didn't know anyone else who wore cap-toe Johnston & Murphy, I was tagged."

"Cynthia - Cynthia, did you hear what I just said?"

"What, oh I'm sorry," sounding startled, "uh yes, I heard you."

"Man, when you zone out you really disappear. So why?"

"Why what?"

"See, you didn't hear me."

"I'm sorry Arthur, I just have so much on my mind and there just doesn't seem to be enough time to get it all done. What was your question?"

"Why two weeks and do you really think I look that good?"

"Yes my darling you look that good, now listen up. The Gaftgo/ Pharmil Pharmaceutical merger is going to be formally announced next month. The powers that be want to review the details of the merger and plans for restructuring the work force – in other words – code phrase for downsizing. Did you forget that I created the new structure and I am responsible for implementation?"

"Not in a million years. How could I forget! Besides every time I pick up a newspaper or turn on the TV that's all I hear about these days. You know everyone at work believes I am married to a real genius and they don't miss a chance to let me know what they are thinking. But seriously, my question was why New Orleans and why two weeks? Gaftgo and Pharmil don't have any companies in that area."

"It's Jason's favorite place, so I guess if he has to spend two weeks anywhere other than on his boat discussing business, it might as well be in his favorite city."

"Your boss really knows how to live, Cyn."

"Look at it this way Art, you chose the Prosecutor's office and Jason chose mega bucks. You always wanted to change the world and make it a safer place for people to live, Jason Benedict always wanted to change his bank balance and being head honcho of MarKinley lets him do it. You love your work, I love mine. I'm not so sure I can say the same about Jason."

"I get your point. Is there anything in particular I need to know about the girls?"

"No, Rebecca and Jean are pretty well set. They do expect you to be home every night by 6 pm to play Mr. Mom."

"I'm not sure I understand or even like the Mr. Mom comment, but I'm going to let it go because there is something I really want you to know now." His large rugged hands reach for her, clasping them firmly around her upper arms he gently pulls her toward him holding her so close she can feel his warm breathe on her face as her nostrils take in that just out of the shower scent.

"My life with you has been terrific. Thanks to you I am where I am today and you have done a fabulous job raising our daughters while developing a great career. I know it wasn't easy and sometimes I was and still am the one causing problems, but I am so proud of you and I love you very, very much."

"Good lord Arthur, you are scaring me. Either one of us is about to die or you are getting ready to ask me for a divorce before I get on that plane."

"Funny, you are real funny! Seriously Cynthia I should say this more often. Our girls are two of the most responsible people I know and, believe me, as Chief Prosecutor I have seen it all. Thank you!"

"No Art, thank us, this has always been a team effort even if you can't remember what I tell you."

Arthur laughing while stepping back, "you just don't know how to let things go, do you?"

"I've had a lot of practice being married to you for 37 years," she says smiling. He slowly moves his hands up and surrounds her face. With his eyes steely fixed on hers, bends his head and places his full soft lips on hers in a way she has not been kissed in a very long time – slow, with meaning and passion.

Pulling away slowly, "well Mr. Farrell, perhaps I should go away for two weeks more often. That was very, very nice, thank you. Just too bad I now have to shift into high gear to get ready or else I will not make that plane."

"All right – if I have to let you go. But thank you Mrs. Farrell. You know for an old broad you are still one sexy momma."

Somewhat amused because it is so in character for Arthur to throw 'water' on the smoldering embers yet dismayed and a bit hurt by his remark, "just once I wish you would quit while you're ahead."

"What, what does that mean? What did I do? I thought I was saying something nice. You are a sexy momma."

Turning back toward the bed to finish packing and not responding to his question, "you had better get a move on, or did you forget that you are taking me to the airport."

"No, I didn't forget but I thought you hired a limo this time?"

"Arthur, if you remember correctly it was your idea to start driving me to the airport. You said it gave us a little more time to spend together and I always thought you enjoyed the time as much as I did. If you want to change just let me know and I promise this will be the last time."

Knowing he should have kept his mouth shut, "no, no that's not what I meant. You took what I said the wrong way."

"Arthur, just get your stuff together. I'm just about finished packing and we need to get going."

Backing away from her, "Ok, I'll be downstairs waiting for you."

As he leaves she forcefully closes the suitcase. Reaching for the handle to lift it from the bed, she stops. Raising her right hand to her mouth she runs her fingers slowly over her lips reliving his kiss, then up over her cheek remembering the touch of his large hands as they held her face. She shivers as though struck with a blast of cold air. Her hand leaves her cheek, rests again on her lips then reaches out for the closed suitcase. Slowly lifting it from the bed, "why can't it always be like that? Just once I wish" -- she doesn't finish that sentence.

"Cynthia, are you on your way down? I've started the car already."

Not answering him, "I guess it never occurred to him that I could use a hand in getting this luggage downstairs. Oh well, some things never change." Answering, "I'm on my way Art, I'll be down in a minute."

Loading her shoulders, one with her handbag the other shoulder ready for a large canvas bag jammed with reading material and yarn for crocheting, ever efficient and self-reliant Cynthia Eileen Tate Farrell, age 58, mother of two, lifts her luggage off the bed and rolls it across the floor.

As she makes her way to the bottom of the stairs she calls to Arthur. There is no answer. "Where in heavens name did he disappear? Arthur!" Still no answer, then she notices the front door is slightly open. As she moves toward the door loaded down with handbag, canvas bag, her suitcase and now added to the load, the briefcase she picked up from the foyer table, she looks outside and there in the car sits Arthur, calmly sipping his morning coffee and reading the morning paper.

Surprised by how calm she is as she views Arthur's morning ritual, she begins to laugh. "Oh well," she says out loud, "that's what I get for being a strong-minded, strong-willed, self-sufficient female. I need to take lessons on how to be helpless and mindless."

Now, totally engulfed in giggles as she remembers telling her mother when she was 11, that she wanted to be one of those women she always read about or saw in British movies who carried a fan and suffered from 'the vapors'. It didn't matter that at 11 she didn't know what 'the vapors' were but she figured it had to be something good because every time a woman started falling backwards while clutching her chest and swooning – "oh my, the vapors," some man came running to rescue her. Her mother once told her, "Cynthia Eileen Tate you must be losing your mind. Vapors – please - colored women don't get the vapors, we don't have time."

Her mother thought she was an odd child, always questioning what she was reading, had a lot to say about the TV programs and movies she watched and never missed an opportunity to tell her what the real world for real women was all about. Her mother's favorite expression - "One of these days you will find out exactly what women have to go through in this world." The more she ignored her mother's stories and talked about how her life was going to be different when she grew up, the more she said "just wait - you'll see what I mean soon enough. Live for today Cynthia and let tomorrow take care of itself."

As she makes her way out the door to the car toward her 'knight and her waiting chariot' dragging more stuff than she will probably need or use, she couldn't help thinking – is this what Mother meant about the real world for real woman! She stops briefly watching Arthur do what he does every single day – focus all of his attention on the newspaper and his cup of coffee. Arthur glances from the paper – "need any help Cyn?"

"No Art," making her way to the back of the car, "just pop the trunk." As she loads her stuff in the trunk, now laughing, she hears her voice in her head, "*when are you ever going to learn. It won't kill you to let him know you could use his help.*"

Closing the trunk and walking to the passenger side of the car, Arthur calls out, "Cynthia the front door isn't closed. You left the front door open."

For a split second she just stands by the side of the car peering through the closed window watching him sipping his coffee and reading the paper, not even considering getting out of the car to shut the front door "okay, I'll get it." Smiling as she moves around the car to the front door she realizes that what just happened was no laughing matter.

Taking the keys from her jacket pocket she reaches for the door knob pulling the door shut. As she aims her key toward the lock her hand is shaking. She pauses for a moment unable to take her eyes off of the keys in her hand and unable to maneuver them toward the door.

"Cynthia come on, that plane isn't going to wait for you," shouts Arthur.

The key finally meets its target – click. Deliberately, she removes the key from the door lock as her hand continues to shake. Slowly she turns, walks down the front steps toward the car unable to let the keys leave her shaking hand and return to her jacket pocket. After fumbling to open the car door she slides into the passenger seat.

As Arthur pulls out of the driveway she attempts to settle in for the 45 minute ride from Madison to Newark Airport. She begins to wonder – *is it Arthur or is it me? Have I done this to myself – what have I done to both of us?* So often while growing up she heard her mother say – "if you want a good job done, do it yourself. You can't depend on anyone else to do it the way you want it done." For as long as she can remember she did just what her mother did, always jumped right in to 'fix-it' – volunteering to help friends move, being their therapist, painting and decorating their houses and never once questioning or stepping aside to let someone else handle it.

Not a day went by without her mother saying "I can't trust anybody to do it the way it should be done. You want the job done right you've got to do it yourself." *Oh no*, she thinks, *have I become my mother? Are her messages so ingrained in who and what I am that I created her life for myself?* People relied on her mother so much they didn't think or do things for themselves. She was the neighborhood 'accountant' because everyone said she was so good with money. She could make a dollar feel like you were spending ten. She was their 'psychiatrist' and 'counselor' and 'fashion designer'.

Whatever the circumstances Mother became what they needed or wanted, yet sometimes acted as though she hated having to do everything. But she never stopped, never told anyone that she couldn't do whatever they needed to have done. As she thinks about her daughters she shudders wondering, *what lessons for their lives are they learning from me? I never understood why Mother continued to do it all yet seemed to hate it so much. She always made time for everyone else but never seemed to have enough time for me. She never said no to anyone – except me. But she continued to accept each day's challenge until the day she died. Perhaps that's what made her happy, what made her feel valued and loved. Daddy was no prize and certainly didn't make things easier for her – yet he adored her.*

Again, thinking of her girls, she shudders. *Have I truly become my mother? Have my life's choices been so totally influenced by her words and actions that I don't know how to turn to others for help or to let them do for themselves? Will theirs? But what if……*

"Cynthia, Cynthia?" Arthur calls out.

Startled to hear his voice, she jumps – "what, what?"

"Are you okay," Arthur asks. "You have that look on your face as though you forgot or just remembered something important."

Stammering, "uh no, no I'm fine. I don't think I left anything behind."

"Are you sure?" questions Arthur.

"Yeah, I'm fine." Glancing out the window as they pass Short Hills Mall, "the traffic is ridiculous today," she says to change the subject. "Route 24 is usually better than this at this hour. At this pace I hope I make my plane."

"With me at the wheel, it's a sure thing. Just sit back and relax, you looked real tense a few minutes ago. Are you worried about the New Orleans meeting?"

"No not really, all of the hard work has been done so there shouldn't be any problems. I.....she stops before completing her message as she watches Arthur reach for the radio to continue the other part of his morning ritual – listening to NPR – signaling to her that he is no longer interested in what she has to say. For more years than she will admit to, National Public Radio has been a part of his life. Over the years his discontent about taking a vacation had more to do with missing his daily 'fix' of NPR and less to do with his work as Chief Prosecutor. Watching as he searches for the station, she recalls how friends they have known for more than 40 years have always laughed when she told them about planning a vacation. Everyone who knew Arthur well wished her luck in getting him away but he would go, reluctantly. The real story is I always had to threaten him with divorce to get him away.

Early in our marriage, like most new wives, I attempted to change his routine. For some reason I believed starting the day meant breakfast together and two-way conversation. Silly me - obviously influenced by my love of 1950's movies and TV programs. Now, 37 years later, the only change in that routine is we are both a few pounds heavier, he has NPR, I have meditation and quiet time – perhaps that's what mother meant about the '*real world.*'

As we make our way through the traffic on highway 24, I settle in to my quiet time. Attempting to ask Arthur a question now, as long as NPR is still on the air would be a waste. All comments and questions will now wait until we get to the airport. Meditation is the way I have found to cope with life's issues, I guess NPR is his.

Getting comfortable for the remainder of the ride to Newark Airport she pushes back her front seat to stretch her legs, reaches for the side lever to lower the back of her seat, folds her arms over her chest and, with a deep sigh, closes her eyes.

Chapter Three

New Jersey - 1949

"Oh Mother, she is beautiful. What are you going to name her?" asks 17 year old Mavis Tate.

Charlotte Tate has just given birth to her 6th child. At 46 and with her youngest now 10, this was a birth she was not looking forward to but no one knew that. "I'm not sure, what would you like to name her Mavis? She's the little sister you always wished for."

"I don't know, I don't know. After the boys kept coming I just gave up and didn't think about it anymore. I thought this baby would be another brother. Are you really going to let me name her?"

"If you want to you can," said Charlotte.

"But, what about Daddy?" asks Mavis.

"I don't think it really matters to him. So why don't you give her a name. Just remember if she doesn't like it, you will have to hear about it for the rest of your life."

Mavis, laughing, "Oh she'll like it all right. I just know she will."

"Okay then tell me, what name will you give her?" asks Charlotte.

"I don't know I have to think about it."

"Well don't think too long Mavis, the doctor will be back soon and he will want to know what name to put on her birth certificate."

"Let me hold her Mother. Once I touch her I will be able to feel what I should name her. I need to look into her face, smell her hair, touch her skin, feel her heart beat, see......"

"Mavis," interrupted her mother harshly, "just name the child."

"But Mother, this is a very special day and names are really important. I want her name to have meaning. A name....."

"Mavis," shouts Charlotte, "if you don't give her a name within the next five minutes you will lose your opportunity to do so. Do I make myself clear?"

"Yes Mother," she answers timidly and feeling as though she has just had a large cloth placed over her mouth. She reaches for the tiny motionless bundle wrapped in a very pale yellow blanket delicately trimmed with pink butterflies and bunnies. As Mavis begins to peel away the blanket her new precious sister opens her eyes. "Look Mother, look," she says excitedly, "she is looking right at me, she is looking at me."

"Mavis, she is not looking at you. Newborns cannot see and her eyes are not really open."

"No Mother she is looking at me, she is trying to tell me that she knows who I am and that she is glad I am her big sister. She's saying hi ......oh, look Mother, look, she smiled at me."

"Mavis, that is not a smile just gas. Please just hurry up and name her before she spits up all over everything. Then I will have to hear what you think that means."

"That's not fair Mother and if she does spit up on me, I will take that as a sign that she loves me too and it is her way of letting me know that we will be good friends as well as sisters."

"Mavis," says Charlotte now sounding very annoyed, "please just name the child."

"I am going to name her Cynthia Eileen. How is that?"

Charlotte looks at her as though she has just seen a ghost. "Mavis, what are you thinking? Why do you want to give her that name?"

"Mother, years ago you told me the story of your sister Cynthia and how you felt when she died when she was just a baby and how much you wished she had lived. You always wanted a sister to grow up with, so did I. You always said you wanted to have more girls but boys kept coming. You never expected to have any more children and here she is. I hope you won't be sad or upset with the name Cynthia, but I think Aunt Cynthia has been looking down on us all along and this is her gift to you – to us. She sent this little girl to both of us. The Eileen part is for Mrs. Wahlstrom, your English friend. I always liked her and really missed her after she went back to England to live. She was beautiful, funny, smart, and always knew how to get things done and everybody who ever met her liked her. Looking at this little face I know she will be all of those things too."

Hesitating for a moment, "well, Cynthia Eileen it is" says Charlotte. "I just can't wait until your father hears the story behind this name. Just be sure you tell him that this was your idea."

"Do you think he will object?"

"No, I don't think he will care one way or the other. But I am sure he will think you are crazy," Charlotte says trying to hide a smile.

"Oh Mother, he already thinks that ever since I switched my major from Psychology to Theatre Arts after being at Rutgers for less than a year. I'm used to him thinking I am not playing with a full deck. It doesn't bother me."

"Here, give her to me" says Charlotte with outstretched hands to truly welcome her new bundle of responsibility. "Let me see if she looks any different now that she has been nobly blessed by the 'Prophet' Mavis with a name that she will probably dislike intensely by the time she is 7 years old," staring straight at Mavis, "sound familiar?"

Placing baby Cynthia in her arms, "that's not funny, Mother. I never said I didn't like my name, I just had to grow into it."

"Mavis, need I remind you that at the age of 7 you contacted our attorney to see how much it would cost to legally change your name because you hated it and, you were extremely upset with him because he refused to take your case. Does that ring a bell?"

"Okay, I get your point. But Mr. Martin didn't even want to meet with me to discuss it. That's why I was so upset."

"Oh please don't make me laugh like this, it hurts too much" reaching for her side. "Well, just prepare yourself. History has a way of repeating. Anyway, we praised your ingenuity, initiative, intelligence and your business-like approach at such a young age. It certainly prepared us all for the beautiful, intelligent and go after what you want young woman you are today. The field of Theatre Arts should feel honored to have you amongst its ranks."

"Okay Mother, now I am not sure if I should thank you or make you laugh so it continues to hurt," she says with a smile.

"Mavis my darling, just keep being you. That's what I've come to expect and that's what I love."

"Thank you Mother dear," staring at her new little charge, "did you hear that little Miss Cynthia Eileen Tate your big sister is something else and she is going to make sure you are too."

"I'm sure you will," says Charlotte. "I'm sure you will."

"Knock, knock, is it safe to come in?" says Wilmer, as he sticks his head around the doorway while the rest of his body stays behind.

"Hi sweetheart, sure it's safe to come in. Come welcome your new sister," says Charlotte. As he makes his way into the room and heads toward his mother sixteen year old Wilmer Tate, the second born and the first son of the Tate dynasty, seems less than thrilled that another mouth to feed has joined the group. Of all of her children, Will was the most vocal and very angry with her for having another baby. In a heated discussion with Charlotte soon after he found out she was pregnant he told her she was too old to keep having babies and it was embarrassing.

"Hey Will" shouts Mavis, "look what we've got, isn't she a beauty?"

"Mavis," calls out Charlotte "for goodness sake keep your voice down. This is a hospital after all."

"Gosh Mav it's just a baby, not like a car or anything. Hi Mother," bending to kiss Charlotte on the check without once glancing at the pink and yellow bundle she was holding. "How are you feeling? When are you coming home?"

"Wilmer Tate, it would be a very nice gesture if you welcomed your little sister by at least saying hello. You don't want her to grow up thinking you don't care about her, do you?"

"Gosh Mother, tell Mavis that's not a nice thing to say. I just don't see what all the fuss is about it's only a baby and we've had lots of those."

Sensing that Charlotte was not happy with his comment, Mavis reaches for her sister. "C'mon Will, say hello to Princess Cynthia Eileen Tate. She...."

"Oh my god," shouts Will not letting her finish, "you named her Princess?"

As Charlotte and Mavis exchange glances they start giggling. "Oh no laughs Charlotte, holding her side, "it hurts, it hurts too much to laugh."

"Will, you must have gotten up on the wrong side of the bed this morning. Of course we didn't name her princess," scolds Mavis. "I gave her the name of Cynthia Eileen after Mom's sister who died when she was a baby and after Mrs. Wahlstrom, Mom's friend from England whose name is Eileen. You probably don't remember her you weren't quite six when she left. But I remember her and I always liked her."

"So you named her Mavis not Mother?" questions Will.

"I sure did. Isn't it pretty?"

"It'll do," says a very disinterested Will.

"Here Will hold her, she smells so good and feels so soft, hold her. Let her get to know you," says Mavis practically singing.

As he takes her from Mavis' arms and brings her close to his chest, the newest little Tate makes what sounds like a gurgling sound. "Wow, listen to that she's trying to talk to me. Walter, Luther and Harrison never did that," referring to his brothers. "Wow."

"I told you she was special," says Mavis as she glances toward her mother who has been sitting quietly watching her two oldest children begin the task of caring for their little sister. Charlotte leans back in her bed with a calm sense of knowing that as long as these two are in her life, Cynthia Eileen will always be okay and the dread of having another child and one at this age, now just a distant memory but a memory tainted with the fact that she did not want her in the first place.

"Has Pop seen her?" asks Will.

"Not yet," answer Charlotte and Mavis at the same time. "He should be here shortly," says Charlotte.

"Boy she smells good," says Will. "Why can't you smell like this Mavis?"

"Ha, ha, that's real funny. She can teach you a thing or two," she answers back.

"Okay you two," calls Charlotte "that's enough. You will have the next eighteen years to worry about how good she smells."

"Well, it looks as though the newest Tate is a hit," says Dr. Birch as he steps into the room. "I couldn't help but hear the debate over who smells better. Now, does this good smelling creature have a name yet?"

"You bet she does," says Mavis. "Her birth certificate will read Cynthia Eileen Tate."

"What happened to the Princess part," kids Dr. Birch.

"Oh no," respond Mavis and Will at the same time, "you heard that too?" said Mavis.

"I did and I thought it sounded really good," said Dr. Birch.

"You're kidding, right?" questions Will.

"Yeah, I'm kidding. But it makes sense, she looks like a Princess," turning his attention to Charlotte. "How are you feeling? During delivery you had me worried there for a little while."

"I'm much better now, much better."

"Good. Let me go and get little Miss Cynthia Eileen recorded and I will be back to take a look at you and we can talk about when you can go home. Just sit back and enjoy these two," pointing to Will and Mavis now standing on the other side of the room. "It looks like you will have to wrestle them to get next to Cynthia again."

"Thank you Jay. I don't know what I would have done without you."

"It's a new day Charlotte, how you felt about this before is in the past. Just take each day as it comes and you will be just fine. I'll be back in a little bit."

"How can I ever thank you for getting me through this," says Charlotte close to tears.

Jay Birch gently places his hand on the back of hers, "Charlotte, you and I have known each other for twenty years. We have been good friends in addition to my being your doctor. You do not need to thank me."

"Yes I do Jay," placing her free hand on top of his. "Without your caring my life the past few months would have been unbearable. Without you…"

"Stop Charlotte" withdrawing his hand, "it was your strength and determination to make it all work. My role was cheerleader and we just happen to make a great team. You know that I will always be in your corner. Now, enjoy your new family member, let Mavis and Will play a major role in her life and yours. It looks as though they have started already," glancing toward baby Cynthia and her big brother and sister as they hold her up to the window to show her what's to come. Gently touching Charlotte's cheek, "I will always be here for you no matter what." Turning to leave as he reaches the doorway, he calls to Mavis and Will, "hey you two, you can take her home tomorrow if you promise me to also take good care of your Mother. Is that a deal?"

"You bet it's a deal" shouts Mavis. "You bet."

Chapter Four

Newark Airport

"Cynthia, wake up! Cynthia," says Arthur gently shaking her. "We're here we're at the airport wake up."

"Oh wow," answers a groggy Cynthia. "I can't believe I fell asleep, I've never done that before."

"Well, there is a first time for everything," replies Arthur. "Come on, I'll get your bag and things. Are you checking anything or keeping it with you?"

"Oh, I think I will check my suitcase this time but I will keep the canvas bag with me. I have some notes I need to look over and I would rather do it on the plane than wait until later. Things might just get a little crazy."

"Okay," says Arthur as he reaches for the door handle steps out and makes his way to the back of the car.

Cynthia remains in the front seat as though glued in place. Still very uncomfortable with the fact that she slept practically the entire way to the airport. She catches a glimpse of Arthur as he moves toward the curb with her bag and calls to a skycap.

"Cynthia. Cynthia," calls Arthur, not sure she can hear him through the closed door. "Are you all right?"

Slowly opening her door, "I'm fine Art, just feeling a lot more tired than I thought I was."

"That doesn't sound like you honey and you are not doing a good job convincing me everything is Ok?"

"Arthur please, I said I am fine." As she closes the door behind her she hears the skycap say to Arthur, "what airline sir?"

She whirls around, "it's Flight 318 to New Orleans" with a hint of annoyance in her voice. "Yes, ma-am" answers the skycap, "flight 318 to New Orleans, your ticket please."

As she hands the skycap her ticket, she sees Arthur staring at her.

"Okay Cyn, now I know something is wrong. I have never heard you speak to anyone like that. He didn't do anything to you. What's wrong?"

"It's nothing Arthur. Well, maybe it is. I just get a little tired of people assuming it is the man traveling for business and not a woman."

"Whoa – hey – this is not you talking. How is that man supposed to know who is doing the traveling, much less, why should he even care? You are more worried and upset about this trip than you want anyone to know or you are not feeling well. But something is definitely wrong."

"Perhaps you are right maybe I am more worried about this trip and the merger. Right now all I know is I am feeling very tired. I'm sorry Art I know once I get on that plane I'll be fine."

"I know you will be. Don't worry honey knowing you every 'I' has been dotted and every 'T' crossed. Just relax and have a good time. This is your time to shine and you worked hard for it. So now that it is here just enjoy it. Just think about me sitting in my favorite chair in front of the television in our beautiful home while 15 news stations are praising the accomplishments of my brilliant and beautiful wife. My chest will be out so far don't be too surprised if a wall or two has moved or has several large holes in it, when you get back. That's how proud I will be --- not that I am not always proud of you."

With a huge smile on her face, "thank you my darling. You are a bit loony but I love you just the same. Thank you."

"Your ticket ma-am," says the skycap as he approaches them at the curb. "Your luggage has been checked through to New Orleans on Flight 318 leaving from Gate 47. Have a very pleasant flight and a good day."

Sensing the double meaning in his message and knowing her behavior was way out of line Cynthia opens her purse, takes out a $20 bill and sheepishly hands it to the skycap. "Thank you very much Robert," having noticed his name plate for the first time, "I appreciate your help and have a great day."

"Thank you Mrs. Farrell and you do the same."

As the skycap walks away leaving them at the curb to say their good-byes "now that's my Cynthia," says Arthur. He leans over to kiss her on the forehead, wraps his arms around her shoulders and holds tight. Pulling away, "you get on that plane, relax and tomorrow show the 'boys' how business is really done. Just think about this, when the details of the merger is the feature news story tomorrow, every smartass in my office will be waiting to say something to me. Knock them 'dead' sweetheart and I'll talk to you tonight."

"I'll talk to you later honey. Thanks again. Bye."

"Bye" calls out Arthur as he makes his way to the partially open door, slides easily into the driver's seat, fastens his seat belt, waves to her and drives off.

As Cynthia gathers her other bags from the curb she wonders if Brooke is at the airport. Brooke Stephenson has worked for Cynthia as an Administrative Assistant for close to five years. She never graduated from college but Cynthia didn't care and ignored the company policy against hiring her. Immediately during the interview, she recognized how extremely smart she was and her willingness to work hard and that she had a great sense of humor and personality. That type of talent is very hard to find so she hired her on the spot. Through the years she has rewarded Brooke's work with appropriate raises and for her work on the merger, Cynthia challenged a company policy that prohibited assistants from traveling, and rewarded Brooke with this trip to New Orleans with her. She really deserved it, she put in almost as many long hours as Cynthia and Cynthia knew she could count on the accuracy of Brooke's research. In many ways, they are very much alike. When she told Brooke she was going to New Orleans she jumped so high Cynthia just knew her head would hit the ceiling. For weeks that's all she talked about. Cynthia always chuckled and seemed amazed at Brooke's excitement, until one day she told her that she had never traveled anywhere, had never been on a plane and this trip would be a dream come true for her.

Picking up her bags after going through security, Cynthia makes her way to Gate 47. Suddenly she feels a tap on her shoulder.

"Excuse me Miss, I think this fell out of your bag during the security check."

"What," slowly turning to look and finding an outstretched hand holding a freshly wound ball of yarn. As she lifts her eyes from the ball of yarn she stares into the lightest brown eyes she has ever seen on a Black person.

Feeling embarrassed, "what, oh my goodness," she says when she finally notices the ball of yarn in his hand. "I'm so sorry." Stuttering, "thank you, thank you very much." As she reaches for the yarn in the palm of his outstretched hand her fingers lightly touch his. *How soft,* she thinks. "Oh excuse me, thank you, again."

"You are more than welcome. Have a good flight."

"Yes, you too," she says slightly stammering as she removes the yarn from his hand.

Man, he must think I'm a real ditz, she thinks as she makes her way toward her gate. *But those eyes, wow, I've never seen eyes that light on any one, almost cat like.* She can't stop thinking about his eyes. Then she zeros in on the fact that he is walking right in front of her. *Look at that suit,* she thinks, *that is one expensive suit. I wonder what he does for a living. I wonder where he is going, what flight he is on. Where he is......*

"Hey, boss lady, where are you going? Cynthia – Cynthia where are you going this is the gate."

Looking around to see who is calling her she sees Brooke sitting in a chair waving at her. Glancing over her head she realizes that she just walked past Gate 47. As she turns heading toward Brooke, she couldn't help but laugh to herself.

Brooke stands as she approaches her seat. "What the devil were you thinking about," chastises Brooke. "You looked almost zombie like walking by. Are you okay?"

"Hey Brooke I'm fine just a little too wrapped up in what to expect tomorrow. Sorry."

"You need to relax boss lady. We are the greatest team in that entire company and I assure you that nothing is going to go wrong. Besides, if it does, Mr. Benedict will probably blame me and that will be the last of my world travels."

Chuckling, "Brooke my dear if the tiniest thing goes wrong during the next two weeks, we will be standing shoulder to shoulder on the unemployment line. Don't worry, I got your back."

Laughing loudly, "and boss lady you know I have yours. Now tell me the real story as to why you were looking like dead lady walking."

"Well at least let me put my bags down and get comfortable, we have at least 40 minutes before they start boarding."

"Okay, while you are getting settled I'm going to the Ladies Room. I have to go bad but I didn't want to leave my bag here. I'll be right back."

"Good, I need to just sit quietly for a minute." Removing the canvas bag from her shoulder she places it in the next seat. As she looks at the posted flight information to double check departure time, without realizing it, the bag tips over a little and out rolls a ball of yarn. She turns and takes her seat between Brooke's carryon and the canvas bag. She opens her purse and the envelope containing her ticket and pre-boarding pass drops to the floor. Bending over to retrieve it she sees a pair of Johnston & Murphy mocha colored cap-toe shoes near her.

She pauses before taking the envelope from the floor transfixed on the shoes - shoes that have always played such an important role in her life. As her fingers wrap around the envelope with her ticket she pauses, the shoes are not moving. Slowly she lifts herself up, ticket envelope in hand to once again stare into the lightest brown eyes she has ever seen.

"I think this might belong to you."

As she makes her way from his eyes to his outstretched hand holding yet another ball of her yarn, to a smile showcasing the most perfectly shaped teeth, she is truly at a loss for words.

"I found this on the other side of your row. I didn't really pay much attention to it until I saw you sitting here. Just a wild guess this belongs to you. If I'm wrong, I'm sorry to bother you."

Stammering like a twelve year old school girl seeing her favorite movie star up close, "I'm sorry, really sorry. Thank you." Now staring at the ball of yarn, "yes it is mine. Thank you."

"Please don't apologize, there could be a career in this for me," he says flashing a broad grin and those magnificent teeth. "Here you go," as he raises his still outstretched hand beckoning her to see that her yarn ball was still in his grasp.

She reaches for the ball of yarn being very careful to not touch his fingers again. Not knowing what to say to him, she utters "thank you."

"You're welcome. Again, have a pleasant flight." As the mystery man walks away, he slightly brushes past Brooke.

"Pray tell who was that, are you holding out on me boss lady?"

"What?" answers a somewhat startled Cynthia. "What did you say?"

"That gorgeous man you were talking to. Who is he? What did he want? Do you know him?" rushes Brooke.

"Uh no, I don't know him. I dropped a ball of yarn and he picked it up."

"Well, let me go find something to drop in front of him. In fact, let me go drop in front of him. It wouldn't bother me at all if he reached down and picked me up."

Now both laughing loudly, "you know Brooke I always sensed you were a little weird, now I really know you are."

"Pray tell what is weird about dropping yourself in front of a man who looks like that and having him pick you up. Or is he only into yarn?"

Still laughing, "I am not even going to dignify that with an answer. Come on sit down, let's talk about what we can expect and need to do tomorrow."

"Aw shucks, I would much rather talk about him," whines Brooke. "That guy is super gorgeous!"

"That's enough" chastises Cynthia, "remember this is a business trip and we are not here to pick up guys."

"Speak for yourself," says Brooke. "I think as soon as we get to New Orleans I'm going to find me a yarn shop."

"Since when did you become interested in knitting or crocheting," questions Cynthia.

"Who the heck said anything about knitting or crochet? If that's the kind of guy who shows up when a ball of yarn is dropped then I will be dropping yarn all over town. You just wait and see," kids Brooke.

"Good morning ladies and gentlemen Flight 318 to New Orleans is now ready for boarding. If you have checked in and have a boarding pass please proceed to the open door. If you have not checked in, please come to the desk now. We will begin boarding first class passengers in approximately five minutes."

"Are we flying first class, Cynthia?"

"Yes we are did you check to make sure your boarding pass is in the envelope?"

"Yes, I checked it before I left home. This is so thrilling," answers Brooke sounding like an excited nine year old. "I can't begin to thank you enough for making this happen. Not only my first plane ride but going to an historic city like New Orleans, and for two weeks. Man, I am in seventh heaven. Thank you."

"You have to stop thanking me Brooke. You are on this trip because you deserve to be on this trip. What we accomplished during the last twelve months would not have happened as smoothly without you by my side. You deserve much of the credit for making me look good. I always said we make a great team, so just sit back and enjoy your piece of it."

"Thank you – oh – I'm sorry I mean, okay partner."

"Good, now let's get on that plane and get ready to have some fun. I promise you it won't be all work. New Orleans has a fabulous history so we will definitely schedule time to see some of it."

"We are now ready to begin boarding our first class passengers on Flight 318 for New Orleans. Thank you and have a pleasant day."

"Where is the place you go for the donut things every time you are in New Orleans? I forgot what you called them," asks Brooke.

"What donut things – oh you mean beignets," says Cynthia.

"Yeah that's it – bennays," says Brooke.

"No Brooke, it is pronounced bei...oh forget it," chuckles Cynthia. "I always make sure to include a trip to Café Du Monde in the French Quarter. As soon as we check into the hotel and get settled we are on our way. It is truly the one thing I look forward to when I am in New Orleans."

As they gather their belongings from the chair and begin to make their way toward the open door to their flight, Brooke grabs Cynthia's arm. "Thank you so much. I know you don't want me to keep saying that but I have never been so excited about anything in my entire life before today. This is a fantasy come to life for me."

"Once again you are very, very welcome. Now, if you don't let go of my arm we will miss this flight and miss our New Orleans adventure. How's that for another chapter in your fantasy?" Cynthia says smiling.

"You don't have to tell me twice," bellows Brooke. "Let's get moving – last one to the gate pays for the bennays."

"You're on Ms. Brooke but it won't be me who is paying," as she nudges Brooke over to try to put her off balance, giving her a chance to get in front to be first to the gate. As they approach the open door at Gate 47 giggling like two 12 year olds and loaded down with various bags of stuff, Brooke eases ahead. "You're paying, you're paying."

"And you cheated," scolds Cynthia.

"I sure did," she says as she slips her arm through Cynthia's. As they make their way pass the flight attendant checking their boarding passes, Brooke yells to no one in particular – "look out New Orleans here come Cynthia and Brooke, ready for whatever."

Still arm-in-arm as they make their way down the ramp, "I'm not sure what you mean by 'ready for whatever' and I'm not sure I want to know," says Cynthia "but the one promise I will make to you is that it will not be all work and no play. There is so much to do and so much beauty to see in New Orleans and I am more than happy to share what I know about the city with you. Let's go get 'em!"

Chapter Five

"Ladies and gentlemen, please fasten your seat belts for our final descent into New Orleans," coaxes the flight attendant. "The current temperature is 77 and, according to all reports, the weather is expected to be beautiful for the coming week. The Captain informs me we should be on the ground in 10 minutes. Before deplaning, please be sure to check around your seat and in the overhead bins to ensure you have all of your belongings. Have a pleasant stay. For those passengers continuing on, a flight attendant will be available at the top of the ramp to answer your questions about connections."

"Oh man," sighs Brooke – "this is going to be the longest 10 minutes of my life. I am so excited, I just can't wait."

"Relax Brooke New Orleans will wait for you. Here, look through this guidebook I picked up on my last trip and let me know what interests you and what you would like to see and do. I'm not sure just how much free time we will have – but we will make the most of what we do have."

As Brooke flips through the pages, not focusing on anything in particular, she hears what she has been waiting for. "Welcome to New Orleans. Please remain seated until the plane makes a complete stop and the Captain has turned off the seat belt sign. Enjoy your visit and remember us for your next flight."

As she glances at Cynthia and gently touches her arm, there are tears in her eyes. Feeling her touch Cynthia turns toward her. Seeing the expression on her face Cynthia can't help but remember her feeling on her first plane ride and first trip to New Orleans and thinking – *I know just how she feels.* Placing her hand on top of Brooke's – "okay Ms. Stephenson, here's the deal – you say thank you one more time and I'm going to make sure you don't unbuckle and leave this plane -- I know the person flying it," she says with a wide grin.

"No you don't, but I get it. Please, just let me say again how much I really, really greatly appreciate this," having a hard time holding back the tears.

With heads bent and foreheads touching while laughing uncontrollably, they are totally oblivious to the stares of the people standing in the aisle over them and the beautiful suit and the light brown eyes four rows back.

Standing and linking arms like two High School co-eds getting set for the class trip of a lifetime, they make their way into the aisle thanking the flight attendant and the Captain, now standing at the cockpit door, and off the plane. Lightly skipping as they head up the ramp, "hey boss lady, can't you just imagine what they would say at the office if they could see us now – most of the people in that company already believe I'm nuts, but I bet they would be real surprised to see you right now. What do you think?" "Brooke," replies Cynthia "this will be the secret we carry to our graves and don't you forget it! "Gotcha – oh wise one. Gotcha!" replies Brooke.

Chapter Six

"What's the name of our hotel?" asks Brooke. "I know I made the reservations but right now my mind is just one big blank."

"The Grand Aldophin and if you can't remember, I hope there will be a reservation for us when we arrive," queries Cynthia.

"If I didn't know better I would think you don't trust me," says Brooke sounding a little hurt.

"Now you know better than that. However, once you found out you were coming with me and everything you are experiencing today, nothing would surprise me. In fact, by the time we leave this ramp and get through the terminal you may not even remember your own name," kids Cynthia.

"Okay, okay, I get it. Hey – look" shouts Brooke. "There's a man standing over there holding a card with your name on it."

"Where - oh, I see him. He's from the limo service the Travel Department hired to pick us up. It's Jason's favorite service so he made all of the arrangements for us. In fact, we actually have the service for the entire time we are here. So any place you want to go just let him know."

"That's great, but I was hoping to do the real tourist stuff – you know, get on a tour bus and everything."

"Well, you can still do that but just in case you would like a taste of how the other half lives, be my guest. Personally, I do the same thing – I get a ticket, ride the tour bus like any other visitor coming to this city for the first time because each time I see something different and exciting for me. Plus I really enjoy talking to the folks who are on the bus, especially those who are visiting New Orleans for the first time. My boss, however, is not happy unless he is driven everywhere he goes. You can do whatever you like, just keep in mind that this service is also available to you. Plus, in case I am not always with you, it might be the safest way to get around. New Orleans has so many fabulous things to see and do but crime happens everywhere and New Orleans is no stranger to crime."

"Gotcha! Believe me I want to make sure there is a second visit to New Orleans, or anywhere else for that fact, in my future. I know people see me as very trusting of everything and everybody because I am so naïve, but I'm not stupid. Besides, I have mastered some of the roughest areas in New York and survived. If I can do that I can certainly take care of myself in New Orleans. Besides, there is no prestige being attacked in New Orleans. If I am going to be mugged or hurt in any city it has got to be New York."

Stopping dead in her tracks, "did I just hear you correctly? That the only city worth being mugged or attacked in is New York?"

"You heard me correctly" says Brooke, with a tone of pride in her voice.

"OK, I don't think I will touch that one. Can't say I understand it, but as long as you do that's fine with me."

As they approach the card carrying, uniformed driver, "Hello, I'm Cynthia Farrell with MarKinley."

"Good morning Mrs. Farrell and welcome to New Orleans, I'm Brad Taylor. Do you have luggage that needs to be claimed?"

"Yes. This is my assistant Brooke Stephenson. It's her first trip to New Orleans and I'd like for her to see some of this marvelous city. I don't want it to be all work for her."

"I understand Mrs. Farrell and please, call me Brad."

"Okay but only if you promise to call me Cynthia. Every time someone refers to me as Mrs. Farrell, I always look over my shoulder and expect to see my mother-in-law standing right behind me."

Turning his attention to Brooke, "it's nice to meet you Ms. Stephenson and I promise I will do my best to make sure you see the best of what New Orleans has to offer."

"Thanks Brad, but just remember, if she is Cynthia then I am Brooke," she says with a new found confidence.

"Deal," he says smiling. "Please, let me take your bags and make yourselves comfortable while I claim your luggage."

"Thank you but we'll come along with you," says Cynthia. "It doesn't make sense for you to double back for us once you get our luggage."

As Brad gathers their carryon luggage and makes his way ahead of them, Brooke pokes Cynthia in the side. "Is he cute, or is he cute?"

"Yes, he's cute - if you happen to like 6'2", curly brown hair, obviously knows his way around a gym, well-spoken with dark piercing eyes like my brother Will, cute. Please don't tell me I am going to have to keep an eye on you this trip?"

"Hey" shoots back Brooke, "all I said was he's cute." Clearing her throat, "and by the way you just described him I think I may be the one keeping an eye on you these next two weeks. Huh, what do you think? Am I going to have to keep an eye on you?"

Reaching, trying to grab Brooke's arm "very, very funny. Yes, he's cute. Now let's go."

"And I thought you said we were going to have fun on this trip," whines Brooke.

Cynthia smiling, "yes I did say we are going to have fun on this trip, and we will. The Mother in me just wants to be sure what is your definition of fun."

Brooke stops in her tracks, "shame on you Cynthia. I know what you are thinking and that's not what I meant at all. He's cute – that's all. Very, very, very cute and, by the way, I can play the Mother game also."

"Yeah, right!" laughs Cynthia. "C'mon, let's go catch up with Mr. Cute and get out of here."

"Gotcha boss, you don't have to tell me twice. But just remember, I got my eye on you. Actually, I will have both eyes on you."

Linking arms, they make their way toward the Baggage Claim.

Chapter Seven

"Mrs. Farrell – uh I mean Cynthia," Brad calls from the front of the car. "We are approximately 20 minutes from the hotel, is there any place you would like to stop before you check in?"

"Thanks for asking Brad, but I can't think of anything right now."

"Oh, oh," cries out Brooke, like a 4 year old with a desperate need to make a fast run to the bathroom, "Cynthia, what about the bennays? Can we stop now for bennays and take them back to the hotel?"

"The what?" quizzes Cynthia, "the – oh I know what you mean. Brad, would you be kind enough to stop at Café Du Monde for beignets and maybe a quick tour of the French Quarter? Brooke has heard me talk about their beignets so much she can't wait until we get there later this week. Actually, I wouldn't mind having one right now myself."

"No problem at all. If the parking situation isn't too bad at this time, would you like to have them there?" calls Brad.

"You know, that's not a bad idea. Run us through the French Quarter first, then we'll stop. Who knows, I may not get another opportunity to do that before I leave." Turning to Brooke, "okay my dear, get ready for a small 'taste' of New Orleans. When you make your plans to tour this city, make sure it includes a walking tour of the French Quarter. It really is the only way to see a lot and to get a feel for the flavor of the area."

"I can't wait," says Brooke barely holding back her excitement. "Cynthia, I will never be able......

Stopping her, "Brooke, if the words thank you are about to come out of your mouth, you will be walking the streets of the French Quarter trying to find your way to the hotel. Remember we had a deal and I want you to stick to it." Softening her tone, "look honey, I don't know everything about your life, but what you have shared with me during the past 5 years we've been together, I truly understand how you feel. But Brooke, I want you to start recognizing just how smart you are, how capable and hard working you are. If you do nothing else for me during the time we continue to work together, learn to believe in yourself. You may not have had that opportunity in the past with your other work experiences, but your parents did a fabulous job instilling in you those values many people today lack. You are the person you are because they focused on integrity, pride in your work and kindness to everyone. I know there are people in our company that see your kindness and trusting nature as naïve, but that's their problem not yours. Once again, you are on this trip because you deserve to be. Every step of the way you helped make me look good and it brought me recognition that made me the talk of the town. The truth is that might not have happened for me without you. This trip is not a charity present or a 'stick it to the company policy crap' about secretaries not traveling. You earned this trip with your dedication to your work and the quality of that work. Accept that and let this be the beginning of the Brooke Stephenson I know and have come to depend on. See in yourself what I see in you."

"Wow," says a startled Brooke. "When you get serious, you really get serious. Here's my promise to you Cynthia, this trip and beginning right now, you are going to see a new Brooke – you may recognize a little Cynthia in her but I'm going to let this trip be the turning point in my life. Your guidance and friendship helped get me to this point and I'm ready to take it to the next level. Baby steps in the beginning but I'm ready to start the journey."

"And you know I'll be alongside you when you need that, but mostly behind you bursting with pride watching you soar," as she reaches out and gently touches Brooke's arm.

"Okay" says Brooke sounding extremely confident, 'is this a cum-by-yah moment?"

Breaking into hysterical laughter – they are completely unaware of Brad at the wheel of their block long limo looking in the mirror at the two of them, until his voice comes over the speaker – "Ladies, I am pleased to announce beignets await you."

"Oh my stars, I can't believe we are here already. Let's go eat," says Cynthia.

The car barely stops when Brad jumps from the front seat to open their door. As Cynthia steps from the car her shoulder accidentally brushes against his arm. "Sorry about that, I'm really clumsy today. Would you like to join us?"

"No thank you, Mrs. Far........ I mean Cynthia. I'm fine."

"Well can we bring you something back," coffee, tea, a beignet?"

"No really. I appreciate the offer, but I'm fine."

"Okay, at least I tried. Let's go Brooke."

As Brooke slides across the seat, Brad reaches inside the car to assist her out. Not sure what he is doing, she pauses for a second and looks at his outstretched hand. Without thinking, she slides her hand into his as he gently grabs hold to help her. "Thanks Brad."

Now standing toe-to-toe, "no need to thank me Brooke, that's what I'm here for."

"And you do it so well," she answers, totally aware she is flirting. As she makes her way toward Cynthia she can't help but wonder if he is looking at her while she walks away from the car.

"I saw that!" says Cynthia, jolting her from her fantasy moment.

"Saw what?" questions Brooke.

"Oh, the gentle slide into his hand and, I quote, 'you do it so well' remark."

"Well, he said it was his job so I just wanted him to know how much I appreciated it and that I agree that he does it well."

Not being able to contain a smile as she steps through the door, Cynthia remarks "why Ms. Brooke, I'm beginning to see a new side to you already-my, my!"

"My, my, my foot" shoots back Brooke. "And just what do you call that little teeter-totter act you pulled getting out of the car and brushing against his arm? Huh, what do you call that?"

"That was nothing at all. It's been a long morning and I was just a little unsteady on my feet as I got out of the car." As they make their way toward a table, Cynthia glances back at Brooke and breaks into a huge grin.

Brooke stops dead in her tracks and sticks her arm straight out pointing to Cynthia, "do you want to know what my Aunt Lou would say if she was here right now? She had a word for women like you."

"What kind of word?" questions Cynthia.

"Hussy – you are just a plain ole hussy," says Brooke, barely able to keep from bursting into laughter.

"Well you and your Aunt Lou can call it what you want, but I call it flirting," says Cynthia. "Just because I'm 58 years old doesn't mean I can't flirt with an attractive man. I'm not ready for the retirement home yet."

"Now what do you think Arthur would say if he heard you talking like this?"

"You've got to be kidding," chuckles Cynthia. "First he would say – go Cyn, go girl, show them what you've got. By the way, I guess you never stopped to notice how he looks at you."

"No way," replies a startled and embarrassed Brooke.

"Way," says a smiling Cynthia. "Look Brooke, my husband is an extremely attractive, brilliant man. Women flock to him like bees to honey and he knows he is good looking. What makes you think he doesn't look back every now and then?" says a confident Cynthia.

"And that doesn't bother you?" Brooke asks embarrassed by the news that Arthur has looked at her in any way other than her working with Cynthia.

"Brooke my dear, if I worried about what Arthur was doing every time he stepped out the door I would be sitting in a rocking chair in some mental institution by now. I have known this man for 43 years and have been married to him for 37 and during those 37 years no one has called or come to my house claiming they have been involved with my husband. If in all of these years he was doing something and I never knew about it, he definitely wins the super prize for discretion. No one can control another person once they make up their mind to do whatever it is they want to do. That's what trust and respect are all about in a relationship, especially a marriage. However, that does not mean that you can't look every now and then at an interesting specimen. Know what I mean?"

You hussy!" says Brooke on the verge of hysterical laughter.

Chapter Eight

"Wow," says Brooke glancing upwards as they enter the lobby. "There must be at least one hundred chandeliers on that ceiling."

"It is spectacular. This hotel is Jason's favorite and it is well known the world over for its service and elegance. Wait until you see our suite," says Cynthia.

"Are we sharing a room?" asks Brooke, sounding a little disappointed.

"Yes we are," replies Cynthia. "Trust me, you won't be disappointed. This is the kind of sharing everyone should do. You'll see what I mean when we get to the suite. Why don't you wait here for Brad since he is helping the Bellman and I'll check in at the desk to let them know we have arrived and to find out if Jason has checked in."

As she approaches the front desk and sets her canvas bag stuffed with yarn on the floor, "Hello Mrs. Farrell calls out the clerk, welcome back to The Grand Aldophin. It's always a pleasure to have you with us."

"Thank you Margie, it's really good seeing you again. How is your family these days? When I was here a couple of weeks ago you mentioned your Mom wasn't feeling well and was scheduled for a series of tests."

"Thank you for asking Mrs. Farrell. I am pleased to say she came through them all with a clean slate. The extreme fatigue she was experiencing had more to do with what she was eating than heart trouble. No one could convince her it was not her heart but now she is a strong advocate for good nutrition and exercise. Also, she is back to her work as a volunteer at the nursing home and planning a long awaited trip to the Bahamas. You know, she was more upset about not going to the nursing home to help out than she was about herself."

"I am thrilled to hear it, please give her my best. Maybe on one of these visits I will have an opportunity to meet her. My schedule is usually so packed there is never enough time for me to really enjoy this magnificent city and the people in it. However, my assistant Brooke Stephenson is with me on this trip and I promised her that we will make time to 'play' a little. She has never been to New Orleans and I would love to take a few hours to show her around. We will be here for two weeks and somewhere during that time I would like to remember that I do have a life outside of work. Having Brooke with me may just be the excuse I need to break away once all of the papers are signed on this merger project. Perhaps, we can arrange a time for me to meet your Mom. I feel as though I know her already. I love her spirit and spunk and at 90, she shows no signs of slowing down. I am so happy she is feeling more like herself."

"She would truly love that, Mrs. Farrell. That is very kind of you" replies Margie.

"The next four days will be crazy, but I will be in touch sometime after that to let you know my schedule and to see what we can work out. Also, I'll introduce you to Brooke in a little bit, she's waiting for our driver to unload the luggage. Since my time will not be my own and the work I need her to do will only take a couple of days, perhaps you can assist her in what to see and what to do throughout the city. This was her first plane ride and other than a couple of trips into New York, she has never been out of the state of New Jersey."

"Mrs. Farrell, you can count on me and the rest of the staff here at The Grand Aldophin to see that she is well taken care of," answers an enthusiastic Margie.

"Can you tell me if Mr. Benedict and the team from Gaftgo Pharmaceuticals have arrived?"

"I don't believe so, but let me check just to be sure," answers Margie.

"Cynthia, Cynthia," calls Brooke.

Turning from the counter to answer her, she accidentally knocks over the canvas bag she placed on the floor. "Yes Brooke, what is it?"

"Brad has everything loaded on the cart and is headed for the door."

"Okay" Cynthia calls back. "I'll be finished here in a minute."

"Mrs. Farrell, Mr. Benedict hasn't arrived but The Pharmil group checked in twenty minutes ago and the team from Gaftgo is here but not Chairman Hoban. According to his latest schedule he is not due to check in until after 7:00," says Margie.

"Thanks Margie, at least this will give Brooke and me a chance to just relax a little before everyone gets here. Please leave a note for Mr. Benedict to call me as soon as he arrives."

"I certainly will," replies Margie. "Will you need reservations for dinner tonight?"

"I'm not really sure what plans Mr. Benedict made. I would truly just love to relax and not do much of anything tonight. I have a bag of yarn with me to work on a sweater I started for my daughter Jean and would welcome the time to just put my feet up and crochet."

"I think I know exactly how you feel. However, I do know Mr. Benedict has reserved the Executive Dining Room on your floor for this evening," informs Margie.

"Hi," says Brooke as she sneaks up behind Cynthia at the desk. "Brad has everything ready to go. What floor is our room on?"

"We are in Executive Suite A on the 48th floor. Here is your key, let Brad know and I will join you in a few minutes."

"Wow!" exclaims Brooke. "That really sounds fancy, smancy."

"It is," replies Cynthia. "It is."

"Okay I'll head up now," says Brooke. "Oh, by the way you knocked over your bag of yarn," as she reaches down to set it upright.

"Thanks. Maybe one of these days I will learn not to drag along so much stuff. I need at least three other hands to manage everything lately."

"See you later boss lady," calling over her shoulder as she makes her way toward Brad, the Bellman and a cart loaded with luggage and briefcases.

"Okay," calling to Brooke as she turns back to the counter. "Oh gosh, Margie I totally forgot to introduce you to Brooke. I'm sorry."

"Mrs. Farrell please don't apologize, I know you have a lot on your mind. I read the paper this morning so all of us here at the hotel know exactly what will be happening over the next few days. This is a big deal for you so no apologies necessary."

"You're very kind Margie," says a grateful Cynthia. "I'll have Brooke come down later and introduce herself," reaching to get her canvas bag, "if I don't see you again tonight, have a good evening."

"Thank you Mrs. Farrell," calls Margie. "Have a relaxing evening."

As she makes her way toward the elevator she hears Margie call to her. "Mrs. Farrell, Mrs. Farrell!" Swinging around, she sees Margie waving two balls of yarn in her hand. Making her way back to the front desk, "don't tell me – I guess they rolled out of my bag when I knocked it over. Thank you for finding them Margie, I would have settled down to my sweater only to realize then the yarn was missing."

"Oh don't thank me, Mrs. Farrell. One of our guests who just checked in handed them to me. He said he saw them sticking out from under that small table near the end of the counter. I realized they were probably yours and rolled over that way when I remembered Brooke saying you knocked over your bag."

"Well, that was very nice of him. If you see him again, please tell him thank you for me."

"I certainly will. You know he said the strangest thing when he handed them to me."

"Like what," questions Cynthia.

"Well, at first I thought he was making a joke but he was so serious when he told me he is either lucky or cursed," says Margie.

"What did he mean by that," asks Cynthia

"He said this was the third time today that he picked up a ball of yarn and in all of his 37 years, he wasn't even sure what a ball of yarn looked like. Then he told me he was at Newark Airport earlier and picked up one ball on his way to the gate and another on his way to his seat in the waiting area. Now how strange is that," questions Margie.

"Well Margie, probably not that strange at all," exclaims Cynthia. "You see, Brooke and I flew out of Newark this morning and as I made my way toward the gate a young man tapped me on the shoulder and handed over a ball of yarn. Evidently it rolled out of my bag going through security check. Today truly was not my day. Then, while sitting waiting to board, I started going through an envelope and dropped my boarding pass. As I sat back up after getting it off the floor, there is an outstretched hand right at me with a ball of yarn in it. I can't begin to tell you how embarrassed I was when I saw it was the same young man who picked up the first one. I just can't believe this is the same young man, again, picking up yarn after me. Now, you are telling me he is a guest here?"

"Yes Mrs. Farrell," answers Margie. "Mr. Tate is a regular guest of ours. He comes in from Chicago at least twice a month on business and usually stays three days, sometimes four. You know Mrs. Farrell if my mother was here now she would say it is fate."

"What do you mean by that?"

"Oh, that it was destined for your paths to cross." That people come into our lives for a reason although we never know when, or why. She is a huge believer in karma and paths crossing."

"Was your mother born and raised in New Orleans?"

"Yes she was," answers Margie.

"Please, don't tell me she also believes in Voodoo?" asks Cynthia

"Well" answers Margie, "she really doesn't want anyone to know, but she does. Oh my, I shouldn't have told you that. When you meet her please don't let her know I told you."

"Trust me, I won't say a word. The strangest thing is not that he is the one who keeps picking up yarn after me, but his last name is Tate."

"Why is that so strange," questions Margie.

"You may not believe this Margie, but my maiden name is Tate."

"You're joking?"

"No joke," answers Cynthia shaking her head and smiling. "If I ever really get a chance to talk to Mr. Tate, we may just have to explore the family tree."

"Mrs. Farrell you are funny. You know, I can't wait to get home to tell my mother about this and ask her what she thinks. Have a good night."

"Margie, just in case you do mention it to your Mother, I'm not sure I want to know what it means," she says smiling. "With my schedule for the next two weeks I doubt if I will cross paths with Mr. Tate again. I'll have Brooke come down to introduce herself to you and Franklin about things to do and places to see. Good night."

Chapter Nine

"Man oh man Cynthia wait until you see this place," exclaims an excited Brooke as Cynthia enters the suite. "There's a baby grand piano in the living room and two bedrooms, each one bigger than my entire apartment, decorated in pale yellow and green with fabulous satin sheets and comforters that look like they have been filled with balloons. I don't even remember seeing a room like this in the movies. This is fabulous, just fabulous. Did you know that the bathrooms have two toilets in them and in one the water shoots upward like a fountain,　and did you see that huge arrangement of fruit on the dining room table?　It would take us three weeks to eat all of that. And there is a regular sized kitchen, and did you see……"

"Hey, hey, slow down partner," says Cynthia with her hands outstretched.　"I've been here before and I tried to tell you when I said everyone should share a space like this. I didn't want to tell you ahead of time what to expect so you could experience it for yourself. I knew you would be excited."

"Excited," yells Brooke "excited! This is way beyond excited, this is pure heaven and to think this will be my little slice of heaven for two weeks. How can I ever go back to my tiny apartment after this?"

"Believe me," says Cynthia "it's not as hard as you think. Just enjoy it for the time we are here and experience a world that many of us never have an opportunity to sample. I told you my boss knows how to live, however I'm not really sure he is happy with that life. I love staying here every time I'm in town. This hotel treats everyone like royalty so it becomes part of my fantasy world and I'm pleased that I have the opportunity to experience this. But I will take clearing the table after a family dinner and conversation with my girls and Arthur any day."

"Okay," says Brooke "you keep clearing the table but I'm going to figure out how I can get this."

"Now you are really beginning to scare me. But let me know if you feel the same after you've been here for two weeks. Places like this are not always what they seem."

"What the heck does that mean," asks a dumbfounded Brooke.

"Just remember" says Cynthia, "we are here to work. Keep your ears and eyes wide open and let's have another conversation about this when we are ready to leave."

"Gosh Cynthia, you sound so serious and a little scary."

"I just want you to keep your feet firmly planted on the ground and not be taken in by the grandness of all of this. Don't get me wrong, I welcome the opportunity to be part of this world and love the fantasy.

But then, I always have to remember the real world and what that means for me."

"I hear what you're saying Cynthia. But just for now, just for these two weeks, can we become part of the fantasy?"

"Okay, I think I can do that. Besides it might be fun. Who knows, I may even pretend to be someone else. I haven't done that since I was eight years old. So, just for you and for any time I am not locked in a meeting with the grown-ups, fantasy it is. We will step into a world made by us just for us."

"Now you are scaring me," says Brooke laughing. "But this is going to be fun."

"It will be, and now that we have planned our voyage into a fantasy world, let's get back to the real one for a moment. The next few days will have us working night and day with tons of reading in order to put the finishing touches to this merger. You do remember that is why we are in New Orleans?"

"Funny, real funny," shoots back Brooke. "Yes, I remember. What do I need to do?"

"Well before we think about dinner, I would like to go over all of the documents in the box we sent to the hotel last week. If you would go to the front desk and ask for Margie, she will tell you where the box is and make arrangements to have it sent up here. This way I can review everything as it will be presented each day. Also, I told Margie you would be down to introduce yourself and that this was your first trip to New Orleans. She will introduce you to the Concierge and between the two of them, will assist you in scheduling what you should see while you're here. Just be sure to let them know what you are interested in."

"She's going to introduce me to the who – what – Con....?"

"The Concierge."

"What the heck is that," asks Brooke.

"It's not a That – it's a Who," answers Cynthia. "The Concierge works for the hotel and is the one person who knows absolutely everything about everything in and around town. Tell him what you are interested in and he will point you in that direction. If you need tickets, he'll see that you get them. Just let him know that you are with the MarKinley Group and what you would like to do while you are here. His name is Franklin and he has worked for this hotel for years. He is a super nice person and has taken very good care of Jason and me every time we are in town. He's also very funny."

"Okay," says a skeptical Brooke "I'll take your word for it. I might as well do that now, so I'll see you in a few. It's almost 3:30 now, what time do you want to go to dinner?"

"I may not be available for dinner tonight. I was told that Dr. Hoban will not arrive until 7:00 and Jason reserved a private dining room for 8:00. Just have the box sent up, you work things out with Franklin and then check in with me around 6:00. By then I should know for sure what plans were made for this evening. I'm just hoping it's nothing formal, I would love to just take a nice long hot bath and get to bed early."

"Okay," says Brooke "I'll have that box sent up immediately. Are you sure you don't want my help with those documents?"

"I'm sure. We did a good job organizing everything for each day before we packed it so just go enjoy yourself while you can. Don't forget to take your room key, if I'm not with Jason and Dr. Hoban when you get back, I will definitely be in bed."

"Okay," calls Brooke as she heads toward the door. "Don't work too hard or too long."

Heading toward the bedroom, Cynthia pauses as she thinks about the young man who kept picking up her yarn and what Margie said about her mother. "Um" she says to herself, "I wonder if there is any truth in what Margie's mother believes. Do people really enter our lives for a reason? If so why him? Who is he? Why me? Why now?" Continuing into the bathroom to run a hot bath she remembers his eyes – so light brown they didn't look real and the softness of his fingers as she lifted the ball of yarn from his outstretched hand, a smile that would surely 'light' up any room, and the shoes - Johnston and Murphy cap-toe shoes.

Chapter Ten

"Hello-hello," calls Cynthia into the phone.

"Hey Cyn, I just checked in. Margie told me you and Brooke had arrived. Is everything okay? You sound a little strange."

"Hi Jason, no I'm fine. I dozed off for a few minutes so I'm not completely awake. What Suite are you in?"

"I'm down the hall from you guys in Suite F. Hoban is in Suite G. We're just one big happy family."

"Very funny, did you make plans for dinner?"

"Yes, I did. I had the hotel set up the Executive Dining Room on this floor for us. Dinner at eight and it will just be you, Hoban and me. How was Brooke's first flight?"

"Great – in fact I don't believe she has actually landed yet. Then we checked in here and she was overwhelmed. We may have spoiled her forever for the real world," chuckles Cynthia.

"Great! She's a good kid and a hard worker. I'm glad you made this happen for her."

"Well thank you kind sir I couldn't have done it without you. Also, at some point, please let her know that you also see her as a hard worker and good person. You know she thinks you don't like her."

"How did she come up with that," asks a surprised Jason.

"Oh who knows – maybe it's because every time you pass her desk or stand next to her while waiting for an elevator, you don't seem to see her. You never say hi, you don't kid around with her like you do with everyone else, you know – stuff like that."

"Ouch – am I that bad?"

"I don't see it as bad – just always pre-occupied and deep in thought," kids Cynthia. "At least that's what I tell her."

"Okay, okay I got the message. Where is she now?"

"I'm not sure. What time is it?"

"About 6:15," says Jason. "Why?"

"I sent her downstairs to talk to Margie and Franklin about things to do and see while she is here. She was supposed to call me around 6:00 to find out if I would be tied up with you for dinner and I haven't heard from her."

"Well she obviously figured out a way to get around town without you. Were you planning to have her join us for dinner?"

"No, it's just the 'mother hen' in me surfacing."

"She's a big girl Cyn and I'm sure she can take care of herself. Look, get yourself together, give me a call when you get the sleep out of your eyes, make yourself beautiful and I'll head down to your Suite. Did the boxes with the files arrive safely?"

"They did and I had them sent up here. That's probably why I dozed off. I've read them so often I can almost recite what's written in them from memory. Everything is in order and ready to go so there should be no problems. What time are you getting here?"

"How long will your beauty routine last?"

"Very funny, you should be on TV. What time is it now?"

"Close to 6:35."

"Ok, give me five minutes and head down."

"Are you sure that's long enough? Even I take longer than that."

"That's because you need to and I have more to work with," she says trying hard to stifle a laugh.

"Now who's the funny one? I'll be down in 15 minutes, just in case."

"Oh, you know me too well. See you then."

Chuckling as she puts down the phone and thinking back on their 22 year friendship and 15 years working together, their relationship has never taken a formal tone of boss and employee. They worked hard to make sure one didn't get in the way of the other and the firm he founded grew to be one of the most influential consulting firms in the world. Their work on the Gaftgo/Pharmil merger is the jewel in their crown. So often she has wished for his happiness but, whatever he keeps looking for, just doesn't seem to be there for him.

"Oh well, enough of this walk down memory lane, I better get ready or I will never hear the end of it." Now, as she stands in front of the full length mirror to assess if her favorite black dress is appropriate for tonight's dinner, the phone rings again.

"I thought you said 15 minutes? That wasn't 15 minutes?"

"Hey, Cynthia what's wrong," asks a worried sounding Brooke.

"Oh, Brooke, I'm sorry. I was talking to Jason earlier and he said he would be here in 15 minutes and that was only a few minutes ago. I thought when the phone rang it was him again. Sorry. By the way, where are you? It is almost 6:45 and I asked you to call me by 6:00. Are you okay?"

"I am just great," says an excited Brooke. "After I saw Margie and Franklin, and they are great, I ran into Brad so we went for a ride around town. Not really stopping to see anything but just getting a feel for what to see later. Then we went back to Café Du Monde for a bite to eat. He's very nice and very smart."

"Okay" says Cynthia sounding very motherly, "where are you now?"

"We're heading back to the hotel. We were so busy talking I totally forgot I was to call you by 6:00. I hope you weren't worried."

"No, I wasn't worried."

"Did you get the boxes?"

"I did and everything was in order, thank you. I've organized and arranged what we need and now I'm just waiting for Jason. We will review everything before we have dinner with Dr. Hoban and his team at 8:00."

"Cynthia since you won't be there when I get back I should tell you I think I saw your mystery man."

"What mystery man?"

"You know the guy from the airport with the gorgeous suit, and tremendous light brown eyes who kept picking up your yarn, that mystery man."

"Brooke he's not my mystery man. Where did you see him?"

"He was in Café Du Monde when we got there. I told Brad I recognized him from the airport as the guy who picked up your yarn."

"Did you speak to him?"

"No way!"

"Oh," says Cynthia sounding a little disappointed.

Sensing that it was time to change the subject – "well get back safely, we will be having dinner in the Executive Dining Room on this floor and you will probably be asleep when I get back. So I will see you early tomorrow morning, sleep tight and tell Brad I said hi."

"Will do" replies Brooke, "I'll catch up with you first thing tomorrow morning. Just let me know whatever it is you need me to do. Good night and enjoy your dinner."

"Good night Brooke." *So he likes Café Du Monde,* she thinks to herself as she hangs up the phone. "My goodness, what the heck am I saying." Just then a knock on the door jolts her back to the business at hand. "Who is it?"

"Who are you expecting?" calls back a puzzled sounding Jason.

Making her way to the door she realizes he is going to have a lot to say about that remark. After all, he said he would be down in 15 minutes and 15 minutes had passed. Swinging the door wide open "hi there boss."

"WOW!" exclaims a startled Jason, "you look fantastic. No, amazing and....."

"Okay, okay you can stop there, but now I'm beginning to wonder what you think I look like on a daily basis," as she slowly slides her hands down over her hips. "Your enthusiastic response is greatly appreciated since I didn't buy this dress with the thought that people would say – oh, you look very nice. At least now I know the expense was worth it."

As he enters the room, "Hey, is that the same dress you wore when we were at Chez Josephine? I remember you looking really good, but not this good."

Pushing the door closed so hard it made a loud thud. "Well thanks a lot, just what every woman wants to hear, that she is wearing the same dress twice in a row."

"C'mon Cynthia, you know what I mean. Plus, I thought women appreciated comments like that – because it shows that we are caring and sensitive and notice things about the women in our lives."

"Yeah, right," chuckles Cynthia. "It's a good thing we haven't eaten yet, I do believe my dinner would be all over this floor right now."

"See this just proves what most men, me included, believe. Women don't really want to hear what WE think they only want to hear what THEY think we should say."

"I'm not even going to touch that one," chides Cynthia. "How is your Suite?"

"Well from where I stand it looks exactly like yours, but you can give me the grand tour if you like. Now, where shall we ......" just then his cell phone rings. "Um, it's the front desk I better take this, sorry. Jason Benedict. Oh hi Margie, what's up? Okay, thanks and please keep me posted. Bye."

"What was that all about," asks Cynthia.

"The desk just got a call from Hoban. He won't be able to get here until day after tomorrow. He's waiting to hear from me so if it's okay with you, I'll go back to my room to make this call and find out what is going on. Why don't you try to catch up with Brooke, let me know where you will go for dinner and I'll catch up with you later. No sense wasting that look – you truly look fantastic and that's not a joke."

Heading for the door, "I hope nothing serious has happened he is such a stickler for schedules and staying on track. I'll head downstairs and wait to hear from you." Making their way to the front door she picks up her cell phone, "and to think I had planned to leave this here this evening. Call me as soon as you can, I'll wait in the lobby."

"I will," calls back Jason as he swiftly makes his way out the door and down the hallway.

Picking up the room phone and dialing the front desk, "Margie is that you?"

"Yes Mrs. Farrell, what can I do for you?"

"Can you tell me if my assistant Brooke Stephenson is anywhere around the lobby? It seems as though my plans for dinner have changed so I thought we could get together."

"I saw her just a few minutes ago Mrs. Farrell and it looked as though she was heading toward the private elevator to the Executive Suites. However, if I see her around the lobby I will let her know you are looking for her. She is a very nice person and very, very funny. She told me this was her first plane ride, the first time she had ever been out of New Jersey, except to go to New York, and how much she was looking forward to this trip. Franklin and I gave her loads of information, directions and let her know she could call on us for anything to ensure a memorable stay in New Orleans."

"I told her she would be in excellent hands once she spoke with you and Franklin. Thank you very much Margie and I'll check in with you again shortly if I don't see her soon."

"You are very welcome, Mrs. Farrell. Enjoy your evening and if there is anything else I can do, please don't hesitate to call."

"That goes without saying. Thank you, good night Margie."

"Good night Mrs. Farrell."

The telephone was barely out of her hand and back on the cradle when she heard a key in the door. Before she could turn around Brooke bolted through the door as though she had just seen a ghost.

"Oh my goodness Cynthia, wait until you look at the stuff I got from Margie and Franklin. I don't know how I will be able to see everything they suggested. They were wonderful, oh I love this place. They treated me like I was a Princess, they......"

"Hey, hey, slow down," cautions Cynthia. "At the rate you are going we may just have to schedule a trip to the hospital because you've had a stroke or something."

Holding up her bounty of information for Cynthia to see, she finally notices how she is dressed. "WOW, oh foot, double WOW, you look like a gazillion dollars. You look fabulous! I love your dress and those shoes, WOW!"

Chuckling, "okay, I guess that is my word for the night. It seems as though that was the key word in Jason's description this evening so I will assume that the two of you approve of my look."

"Approve, approve, you look amazing, you look – well – hot!" shoots back Brooke.

"This is good, in less than 30 minutes I've heard WOW a few times, amazing twice and hot once," says Cynthia smiling. "I accept it all. Now, with all of those brochures in your hand and my original plans for the evening changed, where should we take this hot body for dinner?"

"What do you mean your plans for the evening have changed," questions Brooke.

"Dr. Hoban left a message for Jason that he can't get here for another two days. Since plans for tonight were based on having a meeting and dinner I now find myself with nothing on the schedule for tonight and I have no intention of wasting this look. So, go get changed and I'll take a look at some of those brochures to see where we are going. Besides, what good is stepping into a fantasy world if you can't look the part? No one has ever referred to me as hot before so I may as well make the most of this evening and show this hot body off. Who knows if I will ever get another chance so I'll just think of it as a necessary contribution to a fruitful and rewarding trip for you."

"Is that your way of saying you are doing this only for me," asks Brooke.

"Absolutely, you're the only one who has ever referred to me as hot."

"You are kidding! What about Arthur? I'm sure in all of the years you two have been married he must have mentioned it."

Grinning from ear to ear, "my dear Brooke, the only time I have ever heard those words uttered from my darling husband was one night about fifteen years ago when he put his hand on my forehead, looked into my eyes and said, geez Cynthia you are really hot, I think you have a fever. So please understand, there is hot and then - there is hot. Your 'hot' and Arthur's 'hot' are not even in the same library in the same city, let alone being on the same page in the same book. Now go get ready while I look through the information you picked up from Margie and Franklin. Tonight is definitely our night and if he can, Jason will join us once we tell him where we are going. The plan for tonight is good food, fun and to enjoy this fabulous city. Can you handle it?"

"I meant what I said when I told you I'm working on changing and, right now, I can't think of a better place and time to start. I guess if you are not changing the dress of the night is a little fancy."

"My darling child if you think I am changing this look, you definitely have another think coming. Go get ready and let me see if you can keep up with me."

"You know boss before this night is over I think I might just be calling my Aunt Lou. You don't even sound like yourself."

"Excuse me but you were the one who wanted a fantasy life for a few minutes. What makes you think I wouldn't enjoy one too? Now, go get ready or you will stay right here and watch this hot body make its way out that door."

"Yes Ma'am, you don't have to tell me twice. I'll be ready before you can finish the first brochure." Heading toward her room she looks back over her shoulder watching Cynthia sort through the material she picked up. Pausing for a brief second, she whispers to herself – 'thank you Cynthia. Thank you from the bottom of my heart.' Turning, "I'll be ready in a jiffy," she calls out.

"Okay, don't rush. Remember, in a fantasy world there are no time restrictions," calls out Cynthia as Brooke disappears into her room. With a handful of colorful brochures she settles into the oversized, burgundy suede Queen Anne chair to review what adventure awaits them for the evening. Flipping through Brooke's stack she is surprised to find one for a new Broadway style Cabaret Club – 'Café Firebird'. "Oh my stars, I had no idea anything like this existed in New Orleans. I don't even remember reading about its opening. This is fabulous and certainly points us in the direction for the evening. I can't wait to tell Brooke."

For years Cynthia and Joyce spent many a happy evening at The Firebird Café on 46th Street in New York. The one place you could lose yourself for an evening listening to Broadway show tunes performed by magnificent talent. Cynthia's long time friend Barbara Brussell and her accompanist Tedd Firth appeared at The Firebird on a regular basis, so every chance they could get Joyce and Cynthia were in the audience to cheer them on. When The Firebird Café in New York closed, they mourned its passing as deeply as losing a close family member. Life would never be the same.

Flipping through the brochures, "this day is beginning to scare me with all of this uncertainty. At one point I was dreading losing the next two days because of Dr. Hoban's schedule, now having the time to spend with Brooke soaking up New Orleans history and having a New York City style Cabaret Club here in this fabulous city, is truly the icing on the cake." As she lowers the brochures she couldn't help but think about Margie's mother. *'I wonder what she would say about this day. Is it some sort of divine intervention? I can't remember a day in my life so turned around and outside of my control.'* With that thought a little half smile crosses her lips, *maybe that's the point, she thinks. Just when you think you are totally in control of your life and what you do, something comes along to turn that thinking on its backside. This is definitely a day I won't forget for a while. I can't wait to see what the rest of this strange day has in store for me. I.....* a knock at the door halts her thoughts. Lifting herself from the chair with the brochure still in hand, she crosses to the door. "Yes, who is it?"

"Room Service, Ma'am."

"Excuse me," answers back a puzzled Cynthia.

"Room Service, Ma'am!"

"You have the wrong Suite I never ordered Room Service," states Cynthia.

"Excuse me, Ma'am! But my ticket clearly states Suite A – Executive Floor, Mrs. Farrell," answers back a determined female voice.

"Well, it wasn't ordered by me or anyone else in this Suite," answers a slightly annoyed Cynthia through the closed door. "Please take it back!"

"Hey - lady, I can't do that. Someone ordered this food and my job is to deliver it," calls back a belligerent voice on the other side of the closed door. "Are you trying to get me fired? I'll get fired if I don't deliver this food to you or someone who said they were you when it was ordered? Just open the door, take the tray and I will leave."

Now super angry and not even stopping to think it could be someone who might rob them, Cynthia firmly grasps the doorknob and, ready to do battle, throws open the door. The belligerent voice with its back to her now slowly pushing the cart down the hallway, "just who the hell do you think you are," she calls after her. "What is your name because I will make sure you never work at this hotel or any other again, now shouting. "Stop I said."

Without turning around, the Room Service voice calls out "my, my you really are a bitch."

"Excuse me" shouts Cynthia, "what did you say? Just who do you think you are?"

Slowly turning around, "just a lowly servant, doing her job."

Breaking into uncontrollable laughter, Cynthia has to steady herself on the wall to keep from falling. There before her in the most ill-fitting Room Service uniform is her best friend Joyce Carver. As Joyce makes her way toward her with arms outstretched, Cynthia turns and disappears back into her Suite and slams the door shut making sure the safety lock is in place.

Standing against the closed door unable to control the laughter and with tears streaming down her face, there is a very soft knock at the door. "Hey, can I come in and play?" questions a very soft spoken Joyce.

No answer.

Leaning against the door, Joyce calls out once again. "Can I come in and play?"

No answer.

"Cyn, let me in. I'm going to stay right here until you do. Come on, what happened to your sense of humor? Oh that's right, you never had one. By the way, you look absolutely fabulous in that dress."

Cynthia quickly jerks open the door, unaware she is right up against it and Joyce tumbles into the room. As she stands over her spread across the floor she can't hold back the laughing. "Get up, you fool," orders Cynthia. "What the heck on you doing in New Orleans?"

"Well, hello to you too," states Joyce as she picks herself up from the floor. "And how are you Joyce" mimicking Cynthia's voice, "so nice of you to drop by. How long are you staying?" Now standing upright, Cynthia reaches for her. As they stand in the doorway holding each other as though they have not seen each other in years, the laughing is now totally out of control.

"Oh my stars, now I'm going to have to redo my makeup. You have played some weird tricks on me through the years but this is by far the weirdest. What are you doing here and why," questions Cynthia as they make their way into the room.

"When I spoke with Arthur this morning to find out if you got off okay," she states as she settles into the large Queen Anne chair, "he said you were acting funny and thought maybe you weren't feeling well or maybe nerves about the meeting might be getting the best of you. He also said you scared the pants off of a well-meaning skycap. So I decided to bring you a little something to take your mind off of the events of the week – me!"

"Well, I can think of dozens of other ways to do it," scolds Cynthia.

"Me too, but not nearly as funny as hearing you take on an unsuspecting hotel worker. Man Cynthia, you really got pissed off, and to think everyone believes you're the nice one and I'm the witch."

"Believe me after what you just did, you are the witch! But you're my witch and I guess I am stuck with you. Plus we've been together too long to call it quits now."

"Ditto, calls out Joyce, "and don't you forget it. Hey, wait a minute - look at you," zeroing in on Cynthia's dress and five inch Manolo Blahnik pumps, "you look absolutely fabulous. I haven't seen you in that dress since you bought it. What's the occasion," asks Joyce.

Jason and I expected to have dinner tonight with Dr. Hoban, Chairman of Gaftgo Pharmaceuticals. Unfortunately, his schedule changed and he won't be here for another two days. So Jason and I were going to dinner. Then he called and said he would just order in and to take Brooke out to show her a little of the city. Since I was already dressed to the nines, Brooke and I decided we would make it a girls' night out, dress the part and enjoy a little fantasy moment. Besides, Brooke told me I looked hot. So in a brief weak moment, I decided I would take this hot body somewhere and Brooke and I would show it off."

"Well, listen to you," states a surprised Joyce. "We have been close friends for more years than I care to admit to and I have never heard you sound like that. I like this you. It must be the dress."

"Actually," says an equally surprised Cynthia, "I think it's the shoes. Hey, how long are you staying?"

"My original game plan was to surprise you, find out what had Arthur so concerned about you spend the night and take off early tomorrow. Now I'm not so sure I should leave you looking as you do and sounding as you do."

"Does that mean you'll stay around for a while?"

"Well, maybe another day. Besides, I've never been known to turn down a girls' night out before. I can't believe I would begin now at this age. Do you think you and Brooke can handle the competition?"

"Bring it on Miss Thing," kids Cynthia. "I don't know about Brooke but I'm ready to challenge you."

"What about Brooke?" As Cynthia and Joyce turn toward the voice on the other side of the room, their mouths drop open as they stare at an amazing figure in a bright red dress barely covering her thighs, softly draped around a low-cut bust line and neatly cinched at what looks to be a 19 inch waist. Her long hair loosely pulled back with curls carefully framing her face. In a very soft and sultry voice, "did I hear my name mentioned," asks Brooke.

Cynthia slowly turns to Joyce, "what was that you were saying about competition?" No reply. "Oh my goodness" needles Cynthia, "I do believe my dear friend is speechless." She could barely get the words out before laughing and calling out to Brooke, "you go girl. Show these old broads how it's done."

"I guess that means this is okay to wear tonight," questions Brooke.

"Well, like I said earlier, what good is having a fantasy evening if you can't dress the part? You better believe it is okay. It is better than okay, you look absolutely stunning," turning to Joyce "your turn! Let's see what you come up with to outdo the two of us."

"Uh, that's not fair. However, I do have a little something up my sleeve or should I say in my travel bag. My bag is under the cart in the hallway. You ladies of the evening just sit quietly and calm yourselves while this long time diva shows you how it is really done." As Joyce heads for the door Brooke whispers to Cynthia, "I thought ladies of the evening was not a good thing? You know, like hookers" questions Brooke.

"Well who knows? After all this is our fantasy," replies Cynthia.

"That's it," responds a very surprised Brooke "now I know I am going to have to call my Aunt Lou."

As Joyce steps back into the room, travel bag in hand, "what are the two of you whispering about? Do you think I can't overshadow the two of you?"

"Not at all," answers Cynthia. "Brooke just asked me if you were referring to us as hookers."

"What the heck does that mean?" shoots back a startled Joyce.

"Well, you did refer to us as ladies of the evening. In some circles that means something very different than three charming ladies going out for the evening."

"Boy oh boy, now I know I had better stick around for a couple of days. Either the two of you are just over worked or you are losing your minds behind the work you've done on this merger. However, if the shoe fits........"

Before she can finish that sentence, Cynthia picks up a handful of brochures and throws them at her. "Go get dressed and let's get out of here. There is a New York style Cabaret Club with our name all over it and tonight offering the best of Cole Porter."

"How romantic – now whose room am I using to change," asks Joyce as she slings her travel bag over her shoulder.

"Use mine," says Cynthia pointing toward the narrow corridor leading to the grand master suite. "I don't think I want to expose Brooke to your sloppy ways."

"Very funny Mrs. Farrell. I will see you in twenty minutes."

"Please make sure it is only twenty minutes. It is now 7:20, the show starts at 9:00 and I would like to eat before."

"Does this Firebird serve food like the one in New York," asks Joyce.

"It does and we have a reservation for 8. So get a move on."

"Good heavens Cynthia, you sounded just like your mother just then."

"Just go get dressed. It will take us approximately 10 minutes to get there."

"Okay - going, going, gone," as she heads toward Cynthia's room.

Turning toward Brooke as Joyce makes her way down the narrow corridor. "Brooke you look absolutely amazing. I love that dress."

"I'm glad you like it. I bought it six months ago never knowing if I would ever have a chance to wear it. I saw it in a magazine, found it in Nordstrom and thought – maybe one day. Little did I know this would be the day."

"Well, it looks as though Nordstrom has been very good for both of us. Now let's see what Madam Carver comes out in. I'm certain she got her outfit at Nordstrom also. She buys all of her clothes there."

"Gosh" says Brooke, "I wish I could. I've been eating franks and beans everyday to get back what I paid for this one."

"Well, just let me say it was well worth the cost. I'm going to call for Brad and have him ready to leave as soon as we get downstairs. The Club is about 10 minutes from the hotel."

As she finishes her call to Brad that all too familiar voice calls out, "ready or not here I come." Turning around she comes face to face with Joyce in the most drop-dead, gorgeous dress she has ever seen. A pale green silk jersey very high on the neck in the front, and as Joyce twirls around, the back is cut so low and draped in a way that you have no trouble seeing where her back ends and the other part of her anatomy begins. The pale green against her chocolate brown skin, she was heart stopping beautiful. No one would ever believe she is 60 years old.

"Well, by the startled look on your faces I guess I won the 'who has it all together bet' -- right?"

Chapter Eleven

As the car pulls up to Café Firebird "Brad, are you sure you won't join us for the evening? You're more than welcome."

Stepping out of the car to assist them, "I appreciate the offer Cynthia, but no thank you. What time would you like me to return for you?"

"The show ends at 11:00."

"I will be here at 11:00. I hope everyone has a great time."

"Thanks Brad," they call back almost in unison. "See you later."

Entering the Firebird, "my goodness Cyn, this one is as elegant as New York. I always loved the black and white with touches of red. It is so theatrical, so New York."

"I know. Joyce we are definitely going to have to make this a regular stop on our travels."

"Good evening ladies and welcome to Café Firebird."

"Good evening," responds Cynthia, "reservation for Farrell."

"Yes, right this way."

As they enter the main room, Cole Porter's 'De-Lovely' is playing and their table is close enough to the stage and performers ensuring they won't miss a thing and setting the tone for what they know will be a fun evening.

As they settle in and order dinner, Brooke grabs Cynthia's arm. "Cynthia, look, look across at that table, isn't that your mystery man?"

Joyce shifts around in her seat to see what Brooke is talking about. "What mystery man, where?"

"Over there" points Brooke, "the table almost directly across the dance floor from us. That's Cynthia's mystery man."

"Okay Brooke, enough of this nonsense. He is not my mystery man. I don't even know him."

As Joyce leans across the table toward her, "okay my dear friend, spill. Who is this character Brooke is referring to and what does he have to do with you?"

"Oh come on Joyce, I don't even know him. I saw him for the first time this morning at Newark Airport after I dropped a ball of yarn and he picked it up. That's all."

"Well, why does Brooke refer to him as your mystery man?"

Before she has a chance to answer Brooke chimes in, "it wasn't just one time he picked up her yarn, it happened twice at the airport and once at the hotel. Isn't he gorgeous? His light brown eyes are unbelievable."

"Tell me more," encourages Joyce. As they lean toward each other Cynthia glances in his direction, unaware that he has been staring at her for some time. As their eyes meet he gently nods his head acknowledging her presence. Feeling flushed, she is embarrassed by her feelings knowing he is watching her. Yet, she can't bring herself to look away.

"Earth to Cynthia - earth to Cynthia," calls Joyce.

"What," sounding startled.

"Our food is here. Where did you zone out to?" asks Joyce.

"Don't be silly - let's eat," changing the subject. As she reaches for her fork, once again she can't resist looking in his direction and to her great surprise and pleasure, he is looking back.

As the tables are cleared, the band begins to play. "Ladies and gentlemen I am Rex Lauri and I am pleased to welcome you to a very special evening at Café Firebird showcasing the music of the amazing Cole Porter. Before our singers take the stage, please feel free to enjoy the dance floor."

"Cynthia, this is great. Did you know dancing was allowed?" asks Joyce.

"No, I didn't. I don't remember reading that in the brochure. I just thought it would be like the New York Firebird – only performers. This is terrific but now I'm sorry my boss didn't join us. I'm not ready for the old lady dance club just yet."

"What does that mean?" asks Brooke.

"Don't tell me you haven't seen or experienced this at a wedding or social event. It's where all the old ladies get up and dance with each other because, either the old men present won't dance or can't dance. So much for women living longer than men," answers Joyce.

"You're kidding, right?" asks Brooke.

"Nope, you have not lived until you see a dance floor filled with blue haired ladies leading each other across the dance floor," shoots back

Joyce. "But this old lady is very, very different. I guarantee you that before this evening ends, I will have whirled around this floor to the romantic tunes of Mr. Porter with someone in trousers."

"Now, that's a sight I don't intend to miss," kids Brooke. "I can't wait."

"Don't worry my sweet you will be right alongside me. In these dresses any man under the age of 80 would be crazy not to take us on and, if they don't ask us, we will certainly ask them. I am well-known for my technique in picking up men."

Staring at Joyce in utter amazement, "Cynthia, is she serious?"

"Only time will tell. Women have been known to do some strange stuff when they punch the desperate button." As she answers Brooke, she can't keep her eyes away from his table across the dance floor. Once again, her eyes are locked on his. As he pushes back his chair her heart begins to beat a little faster. Is he…..she thinks…..will he…..no, no, what am I doing? Shifting her attention to Joyce, "Joyce, I'm beginning to think you might be more of an influence on Brooke than she needs right now."

"Says who" questions Joyce, "and is that a good thing or a bad thing? Come on Cynthia, this is not the time to get serious and motherly, I thought this was the beginning of our fantasy evening. Maybe Brooke and I should have left you back at the hotel. Besides, this was your idea Mrs. Farrell, don't chicken out on us now."

"That's right Cynthia, I thought a fantasy evening would mean that we would do things that we ordinarily wouldn't do."

"Oh no" sighs Cynthia, "it is bad enough to have Joyce talking like that but now with both of you on the same side this so-called fantasy evening may have things in store for us we didn't plan on."

"Let's hope so but what you just said makes no sense at all," laughs Joyce. "Who ever heard of fantasy adventure details being planned in advance? My idea of a fantasy is you just go with the flow. Make it up as you go along. Call it as you see it-play along. Do what feels right, not do what is right. If we focus on doing what is right it's not a fantasy evening, it's our normal everyday lives. I don't know about you, but I am more than ready to step out of my normal everyday life. In fact it wouldn't hurt you any to step out of yours – Miss do the right thing every time, all the time."

"All right, all right, I don't need a building to fall on me to get the message. You're right – I'm ready, I'm dressed, I'm….."

"Good evening. I hope I'm not intruding," says the voice from the side.

Without thinking they each look up at the same time in the exact same way unable to speak one word.

Looking directly at Cynthia, "I'm Russell Tate or Rusty to my friends. I don't mean to intrude but I feel as if I know you thanks to the yarn balls I've retrieved throughout the day."

For the first time since they sat down, they are speechless.

"Please forgive me if I am interrupting but when I saw you sitting here and recognized you as the 'yarn lady' I thought I should come introduce myself."

"No need to apologize," replies Cynthia. "I'm sorry I didn't recognize you and no, you are not interrupting." *Oh my stars,* she thinks, *how stupid. He knows I recognized him. What a dumb thing to say.* Just then she hears Joyce, "of course you are not interrupting, Rusty. Please join us." As she pulls out a chair, "I'm Joyce Carver, this is Brooke

Stephenson, and the yarn lady is Cynthia Farrell. Tell me again how the two of you met?" quizzes Joyce.

Cynthia quickly shoots her a look as if to say – 'how dare you.' Before he can respond to Joyce's question, "let me thank you again for rescuing my yarn," says Cynthia, trying to sound very casual.

"Please, no thanks necessary, I learned about yarn today for the first time in my life. What brings you to Cafe' Firebird? Are you fans of Cole Porter?"

"Yes, very much so, Joyce and I spent many evenings at a Cabaret Club in Manhattan very similar to this one. What about you?"

"Oh, I've been a huge fan of Cole Porter's for as long as I can remember. He was one of my Mother's favorites and she never missed an opportunity to play his songs and insist my Dad join her on the 'dance' floor – in reality, our dining room. At any given time you could enter my house and watch my parents dancing cheek to cheek with all of the dining room furniture pushed against the wall. They were a little weird that way."

"Oh, how sweet," says Joyce. "More people should be a little weird that way."

Just then the band begins to play 'You'd Be So Easy To Love.' As Rusty swings around in his chair to look at the orchestra, Joyce and Brooke are signaling her to ask him to dance. As she sits there shaking her head no he turns back around – "Would you care to dance?"

Surprised by his question she just stares at him for a minute. "Uh, yes, thank you." As he leads her to the dance floor, he reaches back to take her hand. Sliding her hand into his she recalls the softness of his fingers as she reached for her ball of yarn earlier at Newark Airport. Now, with his hand clasped firmly around hers as they step onto the dance floor, he turns to her and slowly slides his right hand around her waist gently pulling her closer to him. Sensing that she is a little uneasy by his touch, "I'm sorry" he whispers softly in her ear. "I'm so used to dancing with my Mom, I sometimes forget."

Not wanting him to know just how uneasy she is being this close to him - a total stranger - with feelings she can't explain, "please don't apologize, I'm just out of practice. It's been many, many years since I've been on a dance floor like this. Changing the subject to ease the tension, "what brings you to New Orleans, Mr. Tate?"

"Please, Mr. Tate was my Dad I answer only to Russell or Rusty."

Smiling, and beginning to relax a little, "okay Rusty. By the way, my maiden name is Tate. I wonder if we should examine the family tree."

Laughing, "are you kidding, Tate really is your maiden name?"

"Oh yes, I wouldn't make that one up. So what brings you to New Orleans?"

"I'm in New Orleans just about every month these days, so its business as usual."

"So what business as usual do you do?" Trying very hard to sound casual yet feeling very relaxed and comfortable caught in his firm grasp as the vocalist begins to sing – "You'd be so easy to love, so easy to idolize all others above. So worth the yearning for........"

"Cynthia, Cynthia, are you okay?"

"What!" startled by the sound of his voice so close to her ear.

"Are you all right?"

"Yes, yes, I'm fine. I couldn't help getting lost in the lyrics of this song. I'm sorry."

"No need to apologize. If more people got lost in the lyrics of songs like this, I believe it would be a more peaceful world. I was afraid I was boring you with talk of business."

Feeling extremely embarrassed, "please forgive me."

"There's nothing to forgive," as he gently tightens his grasp around her waist.

"Let's try this again, what business as usual do you do?" As she pulls back a little and looks directly into those unbelievable light brown eyes they both start giggling like two newly introduced teenagers, totally unaware of the looks they are getting from others on the dance floor and the quizzical looks from Joyce and Brooke.

"I'm an attorney, I'm based in Chicago and acquisitions and mergers are my game."

You aren't by any chance involved with the Gaftgo/Pharmil merger are you, pulling back to look directly into his amazing eyes. "No, but I've been reading about it. Why do you ask?"

"That's why I'm here."

"Are you an attorney?"

"No, I'm with MarKinley, we developed the restructuring plan."

"I'm impressed," he says with a continuous nod of his head. "What role did you play?"

"I headed the strategic development team."

Forgetting they were on the dance floor, he stops dancing. "Well, now I really am impressed. The Wall Street Journal detailed key elements of the process and hailed it as innovative and brilliant. Who came up with the initial approach?"

Somewhat sheepishly, "I did."

Stepping back and looking directly at her, "and to think when I first saw you I thought you were just another pretty face."

"Lawyer Tate that is one crappy pickup line and you should retire it real, real fast," trying hard to not laugh in his face.

Laughing, "Okay I'm teasing, but I really am impressed. I would like to hear more."

"Sorry, all details are confidential, you are not a member of the press and this is not a corporate board room. So that makes me officially off duty."

"Ouch!"

As they continue to talk and hold each other, swaying back and forth, they are oblivious to the fact that the musicians are no longer playing and everyone else has left the dance floor. Joyce approaches and taps her on the shoulder.

"Uh, excuse me, in case you haven't noticed the music stopped and you are alone on the dance floor."

As they leave the dance floor trying to hide their extreme embarrassment, the room breaks into applause.

"They must think you two are part of the show," says Joyce as she turns around and bows to the crowd.

As Cynthia takes her seat, "you know Cynthia," says Brooke, "I am really sorry I left my cell phone in the room. This definitely calls for getting my Aunt Lou on the phone."

"Very, very funny," replies Cynthia with just a hint of sarcasm.

"Ladies, enjoy your evening and Cynthia, thank you this was fun."

"Wait a minute" shouts Brooke, "you're not going to enjoy the show with us?"

"No Brooke, but thanks for the invitation."

"Cynthia," gently placing his hand on her shoulder, "I hope to see you again and thank you for letting me join the group. Take care everyone and I look forward to the next time."

As Joyce approaches the table and sees him turn to leave, "hey, where are you going? I thought you would hang out with us for the evening. You're not leaving, are you?"

"I am but I truly enjoyed meeting all of you, good-night Joyce."

"Not so fast Mr. I'm not going to let you get away so quickly. Just look around this room. What do you see?"

"A room full of people ready to enjoy a good time."

"That's what I thought. Well, I am one of those people ready to have a good time. Plus you can count on one hand the number of men in this room and since dancing is part of the evening, I have no intention of wasting this great music and this look in the arms of one of those blue haired ladies. Besides, watching you with Cynthia on the dance floor, you look like you were born to dance and just a few minutes ago you told us how much you love Cole Porter's music. So, unless there is an emergency out there tonight that calls for someone with your background you're mine for the next hour or so -- any questions?"

As Rusty glances toward Cynthia with hands outstretched signaling, *'what do I do now?'* she gives him a slight nod that it is okay.

"Well Joyce, it looks like you win. By your tone I guess I couldn't leave right now even if there was an emergency until we circle that dance floor a few times," grinning from ear to ear.

"You're a smart man Mr. Tate, a very smart man." As he pulls back her chair the band begins to play DeLovely.

"Well, listen to that. What about it Miz J, want to show the blue haired ladies how it's done," he asks playfully.

"Are you sure this tune isn't too fast for you," jokingly.

"Just watch me - you better hope you can keep up with me!"

"Now that's a challenge I like. As I said before Mr. Tate, you are a smart man - a very smart man."

While Brooke and Cynthia stare in amazement at the two of them, Joyce and Rusty head toward the dance floor and immediately break into a fox trot looking like contestants vying for the top prize at the National Ballroom Dancing Competition.

"Well, look at that?" quizzes a surprised Brooke.

"Wow! I would have never guessed. They look fabulous." Staring at them and beginning to feel just a tad jealous, "they really are fantastic. I don't think I've ever seen Joyce dance so well or look so beautiful."

"They do dance great together. They remind me of Fred Astaire and Ginger Rodgers," answers Brooke.

"Well, I'm not so sure I would go that far but they do look great together."

"Hey" responds Brooke, "do you know if Rusty is married or something?"

"How the heck would I know I just met him, just like you," trying to sound surprised by Brooke's question yet knowing she asked herself the very same question.

"I sure hope he sticks around long enough for us to dance with him. Oh, I forgot you already did. Well, I hope my turn is next. I can't dance like you and Joyce but I wouldn't mind having him hold me for a few minutes like he held you and now Joyce."

"Brooke," shoots back Cynthia. "I can't believe you just said that."

"Oh come on Cynthia, don't tell me you didn't like the way he held you when you were dancing with him. At least from where I was sitting it sure looked like you did."

"That's just dancing Brooke, nothing more, nothing special." As she heard the words come out of her mouth even she didn't believe them. *Why should Brooke believe me, she questions, when I can't even convince myself.* Staring back at Joyce and Rusty gliding around the floor like dance champions, she had to admit she was jealous – but why! *Remembering - as he gently slipped his arm around my waist and pulled me close, I liked it. The soft, sweet smell of his cologne, the way he closed his large strong, yet soft hand around my hand holding it close to his chest – so close I could feel the beating of his heart. The way my body fit into his like we were two pieces in a jig saw puzzle.*

"Gosh, that was beautiful," says Brooke.

"What, what did you say?" responds a startled Cynthia.

"Gosh Cynthia, where did you disappear to? I said to you three times, they look so beautiful, I love the way they dance. You didn't hear me, did you?"

Very embarrassed, "I heard you Brooke I just didn't think it required a response."

"Yeah right, you know you didn't hear me. You were not paying attention even though you were staring right at them the whole time. If I didn't know better I would think you were jealous of how great they look together."

"I am not even going to dignify that with a response."

"Whatever you say, oh here they come. Please, please, I hope he asks me to dance next."

"Well Brooke, if you want a dance so much and he doesn't ask you, you just ask him."

"You know what Cynthia, that's a great idea. Watch me."

"I feel change in the air already," kids Cynthia.

As Rusty and Joyce approach the table, "Cynthia this guy is terrific. I can't remember the last time I had so much fun on the dance floor."

"You guys looked fabulous out there," chimes Brooke. "I bet everyone here thinks you are professional dancers. You looked like you've been doing this for years and Rusty, where did you learn to dance like that?"

Reaching to pull out Joyce's chair, "Thanks for the compliment. In fact, my mother would be thrilled to hear you say that."

"Why?" she asks like a ten year old school girl.

"When my sister started taking ballroom dancing lessons there weren't enough boys in the class for each girl to have a partner," he says as he sits in the seat next to Cynthia. "So one day my Mother decided that I would be Vivian's partner and signed me up. I came very close to running away from home when I heard that, but after I attended my first class, I really enjoyed it. Plus my sister told me knowing how to dance would turn me into a 'chick magnet' as I got older."

"What the heck does that mean?" asks a bewildered Brooke.

"Well, it seems as though there are three things a guy can do and the girls will hang around."

"Oh I can't wait to hear this one," says Joyce smiling.

"It would make a lot more sense if you knew my sister, but I must say her philosophy paid off when I was in high school and college."

"What, what three things," calls out Brooke so loud heads turn toward their table.

"This was Vivian's theory - [1] Football: an athletic jock just has to stand there and the girls come running, at least that's what she told me. However, since I proved to be a class 'A' loser when I tried out for football, it was very clear to me I should focus on her other two theories. [2] Learn to play the piano. Vivian is eight years older than me and told me when she and her friends went to a club everybody hung around the piano player. I'm afraid piano playing wasn't in my future either. After ten years of lessons even my mother decided enough was enough."

"I'm beginning to get the picture as to what her #3 was," says Cynthia.

Cynthia, Joyce and Brooke all call out at the same time – "Dancing."

"Bingo" says Rusty laughing, "give these ladies a cigar. When my Mom signed me up to be Viv's dance partner little did I know at that time just how much I would like it so when Vivian stopped taking class, I continued until I left home for college. Needless to say, I was a big hit at school dances and never had to worry about having a partner. I spent my high school years dancing with my Mom when my Dad was at work or traveling and when he died I promised her she would never have to worry about having a dance partner. We continued to dance at home every chance we got and also proved to be a big hit on the dance floor at all social events. Okay, okay, I know those looks you can burst out laughing now."

"Oh no way, we wouldn't do that," says Joyce barely able to stifle a laugh.

"Oh yes we would," calls out Brooke.

As their eyes meet Joyce, Brooke and Cynthia can't hold it in any longer and start laughing so loud the manager approached their table and asked them if they would hold it down a bit. Now extremely embarrassed "maybe we had better go," says Cynthia.

"Not before I have a chance to dance with Mr. 'Astaire', says Brooke. "Come on partner, after that story let me see what you've got."

Just as they push back their chairs the lights dim and the same man who approached them and asked them to be quiet heads toward the microphone. "Ladies and gentlemen, it is with great pleasure that Café Firebird presents a very special evening of Cole Porter. Stepping off to the side the curtain opens as the person at the piano begins the evening with 'Night and Day'. Rusty whispers across the table to Brooke - "don't worry Brooke you're next on my dance card."

"Okay you two, I hope you heard that – I'm next on his dance card. Hey Cynthia look, there's Brad at the doorway."

"You're kidding," as she turns around and sees him standing at the entrance. "Oh dear, I had better go see what's going on." Just as she begins to push back, Rusty jumps up to pull the chair back for her. As his large, soft hand reached out and took her elbow to assist her up, she couldn't help thinking – *does he think I can't get out of this chair by myself* or *is he just a throwback to a time when men were attentive to their women and there was nothing sexist about it.* Feeling a little ashamed that she would see his gesture as sexist and remembering her outburst at the airport directed at the skycap, she gently slipped her hand into his outstretched hand and slowly raised herself up from the chair. Now, so close and staring into his magnificent eyes, she momentarily forgot why she got up in the first place. Lowering her eyes, "uh excuse me, I'll be right back." *As she crossed the dance floor to make her way toward Brad her only thought was the gentle grasp of one hand wrapped around hers, the softness of the other placed around her elbow and the look in his eyes when he carefully assisted her to her feet.* The uneasiness she initially felt gone the moment she faced him and admitted to herself – 'I like this – yes, I like this very much.'

"Cynthia I am so sorry for the interruption," calls out Brad as she approaches, snapping her out of her thoughts about Rusty. "Mr. Benedict asked me to find you to let you know that Dr. Hoban's schedule has changed again and he can't get here before next week. He left early this evening for Switzerland on a personal matter. Mr. Benedict is heading back to the office but wanted me to tell you there is no need for you to leave. His message was for you to enjoy the next five days with Brooke and to tell you the two of you really deserve it and if he sees you anywhere near the office, you're fired." Smiling, "he also told me to emphasis the fired part."

Hesitating and feeling off balance, "I'm sorry to hear about Dr. Hoban. I just hope it isn't serious. Well, did Mr. Benedict say I could at least call him?"

"To be honest Cynthia, I got the distinct impression that he didn't want to hear from you at all. I could be wrong, but his voice sounded pretty strong to me when he said you should stay here and enjoy the time with Brooke."

Turning away from him to glance at Joyce, Brooke and Rusty in a huddle chatting about something in an attempt to not disturb the singer on stage, for a brief moment she allowed herself to consider what it would be like to take the time to just 'play.' She had not had a vacation of any kind in two years and there is nothing she can do with all of the key players missing. Turning back to Brad, "you know what I believe

I will do just what Mr. Benedict wishes. After the conference Brooke and I were looking forward to just wandering around the city before we left so instead of an adventure on the back end we will shift into high gear and enjoy what we can until everyone gets back."

"Great, at least I feel comfortable that Mr. Benedict will know I did just want he wanted. Goodnight Cynthia, I'll see you in a couple of hours."

"Goodnight Brad, we'll see you….hey, wait a minute. Why don't you join us?"

"That's really very kind of you Cynthia, but no."

"Hey, didn't Mr. Benedict also tell you that I don't take no for an answer very well."

Smiling, "somehow I got that impression on my own."

"Wise guy," she says smiling back at him. "Look Jason is gone, that means you are technically off duty until Brooke and I are ready to leave here. Unless you can convince me that you have something better to do I am insisting that you join us. Why leave now at 9:30 only to sit around somewhere and come back here at 11:00 to get us. You might as well just sit around with us and, just in case that argument doesn't grab you look around, we have fabulous Cole Porter music and after the featured show dancing is allowed. Take a good look, who are we going to dance with? My friend Joyce is here but she's not my type; the generation gap between Brooke and I signals we don't even dance the same way, plus we've already 'picked up' one unsuspecting guy," pointing back toward the table. "So what do you say? What's it going to be?"

"You know, I think I just got the picture Mr. Benedict was trying to paint for me when he said don't let her snow you into thinking I didn't want her to stay and hang out with Brooke. If you don't convince her she will be on the next plane and will stop by the office before she goes home to her family."

"Oh, no he didn't!"

"Oh, yes he did!"

Walking toward him and linking her arm through his "well, with that said, we can't let Mr. Benedict win can we?"

"I guess I should take that as you are staying and during the next five days you will enjoy yourself."

"My dear Mr. Taylor, you can take it any way you like. Right now there is a seat at that table with my name on it, there is someone I would like to dance with again, and I am not about to waste this look and this dress by not having a good time."

"I hope you won't think I'm overstepping my bounds by saying you look super fantastic."

"Brad, for what I paid for this dress, I feel as though I've just gotten a return on my investment. You can say fantastic for the rest of the evening if you like, it kind of rounds out the list of what I've heard so far."

As they make their way toward the table - "what's on the list?"

"Let's see, Brooke said I looked hot, Mr. Benedict said wow, amazing and fantastic a couple of times, my friend Joyce came up with absolutely fabulous. It was certainly a good start to the evening, and I thank you for adding to it."

"No, thank you. Other than Mr. Benedict, you are the only person who has ever treated me like I'm more than just a driver."

"I'm sorry to hear that but my philosophy has always been your job is what you do, it does not define who and what you are. I've known Mr. Benedict for a very long time and I know he feels the same."

"Wow, I like that."

"Well you can thank my parents for that one. In my family you were raised to respect everyone and to not judge based on how much or how little money, education they had or what side of town they lived in."

"Hi Brad," calls out Brooke as they approach the table. "Cynthia is everything okay?"

"Everything is fine Brooke. Dr. Hoban had personal business to take care of immediately so flew to Switzerland this afternoon. Jason went back to the office but insisted that we stay and enjoy the next five or six days until Dr. Hoban returns. At least that's the message Brad just delivered. So in the event Jason expects us back, and we don't show, we can blame it all on Brad."

"You're staying?" calls out Brooke unable to take her eyes off of Brad.

"Sshh, sshh," they hear from the next table.

"Sorry," Cynthia whispers as she takes her seat. Leaning into the table, "I think we had better wait until intermission before introductions, I get the impression we are disturbing others."

"Okay with me," says Brooke staring at Brad.

"Okay with me," says Rusty staring at Cynthia.

"Well, I was just getting ready to tell all of you to shut up any way," says Joyce.

Glancing around the table at each other and trying to stifle giggles, anyone looking at them would think they were high school seniors out after the prom.

Chapter Twelve

"Hey, what do you think you're doing," calls out Cynthia. "I had dibs on that last beignet."

"Haven't you ever heard the expression, if you snooze you lose -- well you snoozed," says Joyce. "I distinctly recall asking anyone if they wanted it and no one responded. So I took the silence to mean, it's mine."

"How convenient, you obviously waited until everyone was knee-deep in conversation." Looking toward Brooke, "did you hear her ask?"

"Honestly Cynthia, I really wasn't paying attention. Brad was telling me why he moved to New Orleans from Iowa."

"Ladies please," says Rusty. "I have never known Café Du Monde to run out of beignets, even at this late hour. Why don't we just order another round?"

"Whose bright idea was it to come here anyway?" asks Cynthia.

"Uh, I do believe it was mine," says Rusty. "While Brooke and I were dancing she happened to mention this was your favorite place and how excited she was waiting to get here. Since it is also my favorite I thought it would be a great way to end a fabulous evening. It never occurred to me it might cause a problem."

"Rusty shame on you," calls out Joyce. "Don't you realize she is pulling your leg? Trust me, if she wanted that beignet it would definitely be hers. If she didn't want to be here, she wouldn't be. Wait until you get to know her like I know her – and when you do, you won't pay any attention to her, just like I don't."

With the whole table in raucous laughter, "Joyce I will definitely return the favor one day for that remark," says Cynthia.

"You know" says a confused Brooke, "I can never tell if the two of you are kidding or not."

"Brooke my dear" says Joyce, "just wait until you've been around us for a while and I guarantee you won't have any trouble figuring out what is kidding and what is not."

"Speaking of being around, just how long have you known each other and how did you meet," asks Rusty.

"I'm not so sure you really want to know – although it really is an interesting story," says Joyce. "However, with another order of beignets I might just be persuaded to let you in on a little secret."

"Well I don't know about anyone else, but this one I want to hear. How about you Brooke, Brad," quizzes Rusty. Before they can answer he swings around in his chair motioning to their server for another round of beignets.

Cynthia looks directly at Joyce with a squint "you wouldn't dare?"

"How long have you known me? Oh yes I would."

As the beignets are set on the table before them, Rusty turns toward Joyce "okay Ms. Carver, you're on. I get the feeling this is a story I really want to hear," as everyone at the table, along with the couple at the table next to them turn their attention to Cynthia.

"Cynthia was 5 years old when we met in 1954," begins Joyce.

"Joyce" shouts Cynthia, "thanks for letting everyone know just how old I am. Remind me to return the favor one day – and soon."

"Oh please," says Joyce, "if I looked as good as you I would be standing on a roof top somewhere shouting it to the world."

At that moment both Brad and Rusty turn their attention to Cynthia.

"Cynthia," says Brad "never in a million years would I have guessed. Joyce is right, you look fantastic. Don't you think so Rusty?"

As Rusty turns toward her and gazes directly into her eyes, "Brad, I couldn't agree with you more."

"Okay you two, let me get on with my story," says Joyce.

"You mean your version of the story," says Cynthia.

"Well….."

"Hey you two" interrupts Brooke, "stick to the issue, we really want to hear this and hopefully it will explain why the two of you are still friends."

As Brooke looks around the table at Brad and Rusty, they couldn't stop themselves from laughing so loudly everyone still in the Café at 1:30 in the morning was staring at them. Before they could calm down the couple at the next table, who were obviously 'glued' to every word being said, added their opinion – "yes we would like to hear the story also. Hope you don't mind?"

Cynthia turns to them, "no, please listen, the more the merrier."

Believing she was serious, the couple scooted their chairs over to the table to squeeze in.

Through the laughter "okay Joyce" says Brooke, "let it rip."

Cynthia slowly lowers her head into her hands in total disbelief that now perfect strangers are about to hear Joyce's story.

"We were both students at Miss Carlotta's School of Dance in Montclair, New Jersey" continues Joyce. "I was 7 and had been a student there since I was 5. Cynthia's very first recital experience at Miss Carlotta's changed her life. Fifteen minutes before Cynthia's class had to be on stage performing to 'March of the Wooden Soldiers' she asked to go to the bathroom. "Okay," said Miss Carlotta "but don't take too long, everyone has to be in place when the curtain goes up."

"I won't I promise," said Cynthia as she scurried down the hall to the bathroom neatly dressed in a pale blue military jacket with gold braid around her right shoulder and grey trousers. The sound of the taps on her new shiny black tap shoes echoing throughout the quiet hallway made her feel like a real dancer.

"I'm a dancer, I'm a dancer," she sings as she pushes open the door of the girls' bathroom. She entered a stall, locked the door and when it was time to leave, couldn't get the door open. She jiggled the knob, no luck. She punched at the door in panic, no luck. "Oh no, oh no," I can't get out, oh no." Cynthia dropped to her knees believing she could crawl out from under the door but the door was all one piece with no space to squeeze under. Sitting on the floor and thinking she would never get out of that stall and would miss her very first stage performance, and no one would see her under the lights and with makeup on in her soldier suit, she began to cry. Sobbing loudly, she never heard the sound of the bathroom door opening.

"Hey you in there what's wrong?"

No answer and now more frightened than ever, Cynthia just couldn't seem to find her voice to answer the stranger's voice. As she continued to sob the voice on the other side of the door came closer. "Hey, don't cry – it's going to be okay."

Silence.

"Please let me help you, I got stuck in that same stall once. How old are?"

Silence.

"Okay – if that's how you want to be, but I have to go to the bathroom now or I'll miss my time to dance. My Grandma and Poppy are out there with my Mother and brothers and they will not be very happy with me if I miss my routine. They even have a movie camera with them. I've never been in the movies before."

Cynthia hears the stall door next to her close. "Five," answers a slow and quiet voice.

"What did you say?"

Now with a voice just one notch below shouting, "Five," says Cynthia. "I said I'm five."

Smiling, "okay Five, my name is Joyce and I'm 7. Let me see what I can do to help you get out, I'll be finished in a minute." She reaches for the door latch, it doesn't slide back. "Oh phooey" she says to herself softly, not wanting to upset Five any more. She grabs the knob on the latch and pulls the door toward her real hard. She can see the latch loosen and easily slides it back. As she exits she remembers that was the problem she had when she was locked in and why Five can't get out.

Standing in front of Five's stall – "hey Five, I think I know how to get you out of there but you've got to work with me."

"What," says the voice on the other side, "what does that mean?"

"I don't know," says Joyce matter-of-factly, "it's something my Daddy says all the time to my Mom. They're divorced."

"Oh," says Cynthia. "Okay, I'll work with you."

"Great – now this is what you have to do," commands Joyce. "Put both hands on that little knob that you hold to slide it over. Pull real hard toward you then slide the latch at the same time. Got it?"

"I got it," says Cynthia. "Oh no, my hands keep slipping" cries Cynthia.

"Well, they are probably a little sweaty – so rub them together and try again," says Joyce sounding very grownup.

"Okay, here goes." Click. "I did it, I did it," screams a very happy Cynthia as she pushes open the door and rushes out of the stall so fast she practically knocks Joyce over.

"Hey Five slow down," says Joyce and noticing her uniform. "Well, look at you all dressed up like a tin soldier."

"My class is doing March of the Wooden Soldiers," says an excited Cynthia and showing no signs of having been locked in the stall.

"I know," says Joyce.

"How do you know?" quizzes Cynthia.

"Every first year group at Miss Carlotta's does it. I'll let you in on a little secret," says Joyce.

"What, what," says a wide-eyed Cynthia staring up at her rescuer.

"I looked just like you when I was five and it was my first year at Miss Carlotta's. 'March of the Wooden Soldiers' is still my favorite dance," smiling as she reaches for her hand. "Okay Five, we better get going or we'll both be in trouble."

Taking Joyce's hand as they head toward the door, "Cynthia," says the soft voice.

"What?" says Joyce, turning to look at her and forgetting she never said what her name was.

"Cynthia, my name is Cynthia."

As they stroll down the hallway together with the sound of their tap shoes making music of their own, Joyce squeezes and shakes her hand. "Well little Cynthia, I am very pleased to meet you. My name is Joyce Carver."

"Thank you for saving me, I was really scared in there. I'm glad I worked with you."

Joyce smiles, "I'm glad too. We worked really good together."

"Cynthia Tate," a voice screams, "where in heavens name have you been all this time, your group is already on stage waiting for the curtain to go up. Hurry, hurry," shouts Miss Carlotta, "go to your place now."

"Okay, I'm sorry, I'm sorry" as she runs to her place behind the closed curtain ready for the music to start. Once in place, she glances back to see that Joyce is still standing there. Cynthia smiles as Joyce gives her the thumbs up sign.

"Okay everyone, smile, smile – curtain" shouts Miss Carlotta.

"And I've been giving her the thumbs up ever since," says Joyce as she reaches across the table to take Cynthia's hand.

Grasping Joyce's hand, "and I wouldn't have it any other way."

"Oh, oh, I think I'm going to cry," says Brooke. "That was so beautiful - I just love your story," as she places her hand on top of Cynthia's.

"Your story makes me miss my friends back in Iowa," says Brad as he places his hand on top of Brooke's.

As Rusty stretches his left hand toward the middle of the table to join this new found friendship, his right hand carefully seeks out Cynthia's hand below the table. Turning slowly toward him with a look that doesn't even question his action, he gives her hand a gentle squeeze. Staring directly into those magnificent eyes and not letting go and not caring he reached for her hand, in that brief moment feeling something she has not felt in years, she squeezes back.

Chapter Thirteen

"Are you sure you won't stay another night," asks Cynthia.

"As much as I would like to," responds Joyce, "I need to get back. Some of us have real jobs we must get to and I really only planned this to be a surprise pop-in visit. I hope it gave you an opportunity to relax a little and to take your mind off this merger."

"Are you kidding, I can't remember the last time we had so much fun. You know that's the sad part about being a grownup, there never seems to be enough time to just let it all go. Thank you dear friend for showing up when you did, last night was the best night's sleep I've had in months."

"Okay, are you trying to convince me that it was my showing up unannounced or are you trying to convince yourself that your good night's sleep had nothing to do with Mr. Fantastic Eyes?"

"I'm sure you realized just as I did that there is something very special about him."

"Well, I think I would put that another way," says Joyce.

"And that way would be what?" quizzes Cynthia.

"Please don't take this the wrong way, but I saw the way he looked at you and the way you looked back. Am I wrong?"

"I can't explain it Joyce. I don't know this man at all and if it wasn't for picking up my yarn, our paths would have never crossed. I don't know how to explain what I feel, I only know I like the way I feel."

"Look honey, you don't have to explain anything to me. We're all grownups here and what we do, what we feel is no one else's business. Believe me, I am certainly not one who can sit in judgment of you or anyone else. My only advice to you is - go slow, be sure, be careful."

"I don't even know how to respond to that, but thank you. I will certainly keep that in mind."

"Well, I'm finished with what little packing I had to do so I had better head for the airport. I asked Brad if he would take me to the airport, I hope you don't mind?"

"I don't mind at all. I'm not sure what Brooke and I will be doing today or during the next few days to keep him busy."

"Speaking of Brooke, I overheard a little of her conversation with Brad after I asked him about taking me to the airport and I believe she is going with us. In fact, she was the one who mentioned that it would be okay when he said he had to check with you first. I hope she's not in any trouble because of me."

"Not at all, you know how I feel about Brooke and next to you, she knows me better than anyone else. For something like this getting an okay from her is the same as getting it from me. But if she is planning to spend the day sightseeing with Brad, it means I can just kick back and enjoy this time to myself. It is so rare these days, I'm not sure I even know how or what to do. One thing for sure, after last night, I don't want to see another beignet for a couple of years." Laughing "but I also can't remember when I had so much fun. Thank you for this wonderful surprise. When you unlocked that bathroom door in 1954, little did either one of us know that we would be rescuing each other for the rest of our lives."

"I always thought that's what friends are for. I can't imagine my life without you in it. We make one hell of a team, Cynthia. Just promise me that you will take some of this time you have to do what you want to do. You always put everyone first, now turn that 'help wanted' sign around and point it in your direction. I'm sure before I even step on that elevator you will have everything figured out down to the last second, what you will do and where you will go. One last thing and please don't take this the wrong way but given the looks you got from Rusty and what I saw in your face when you looked back, you may have just found the answer. Don't turn into one of those women who do too much and love too little."

Sounding shocked. "Good heavens Joyce, I can't believe you said that."

"Cynthia, I am a realist and probably the most honest person you know, I love you dearly and you know that I would never say or do anything to hurt you or hurt our friendship. Last night something happened. I don't know what but from where I was sitting something did. I'm not here to determine right or wrong but whatever it is, if it makes you happy – even for a little while, you truly deserve it."

"You know me much too well. Maybe better than I know myself. I…."

Stopping her sentence, "don't try to explain it, just enjoy it for whatever it is. Don't analyze it and don't even look for the why, at least, not now. Who knows, you could sit for the next couple of days you have off and finally finish that sweater you started for Jean eight months ago or you and Brooke could wander through every store in this town to fill up the time. Or ….."

"Or what," asks Cynthia.

"Or – you can spend some time with Rusty to get answers to whatever this feeling is," says Joyce as she reaches for her. Holding her close, "whatever your decision I know you so I know you will have whatever it is figured out before my plane lands. Thank you for allowing me to pop in here unannounced, show off this hot body in one of the sexiest dresses I've ever owned and never thought I would actually wear, and for more laughs and beignets than I deserve. My life would be boring as hell if it wasn't for your life. Live for today Cynthia, let tomorrow take care of itself!"

"My stars Joyce, that's what my Mother always said."

"No kidding and just where do you think I got it from. You know Cynthia, sometimes your Mother made a lot of sense."

"You're a real piece of work Ms Carver and I love you dearly."

"Uh excuse me," interrupts Brooke, "I hate to break up this cum-by-yah moment but it is close to 10 o'clock and I'm sure Brad is waiting."

"Boy how time flies when you are having fun and ladies, from where I was sitting last night, a good time was had by all," says Joyce. "Let's do it again real soon."

"Oh Cynthia, I almost forgot," says Brooke, "Brad asked me to ride with him to the airport. I hope that's okay with you."

"Absolutely, that's a great idea."

"Why don't you come with us?" asks Brooke.

"And miss an opportunity to have an uninterrupted hour or two - no thank you. Actually, since Joyce reminded me that I've been working on Jean's sweater for eight months this would be an ideal time to get it finished, so you and Brad use the time to get around this city."

"No, I would feel guilty leaving you alone," answers Brooke.

"Brooke," calls out Joyce. "Personally, I'm sick of listening to her whining about not getting it finished. You would be doing me a favor if you go sight-seeing with Brad so I don't have to hear about this sweater ever again. Wouldn't you like to make me happy?"

"Cynthia, is she serious?"

"Well Brooke, in all of the years I've known her, Joyce does not say things she doesn't mean. So I second her motion. Go have a fun time with Brad and don't even think of me. For the first time in more than a year I don't have to meet a deadline with a new corporate directive and being away from home I don't have to cook, clean, do laundry or dishes – get my point."

"I get it, I don't need to have a building fall on me to see that you prefer a little time to yourself. Or, are the two of you just pushing me toward Brad."

Looking at Joyce startled "my goodness. Joyce do you believe this child thinks we would do such a horrible thing. Forcing her to spend time with one of the most gorgeous, tall, smart, funny young men we've met in a long time. What a horrible punishment for her and we should be punished just for thinking of such a thing."

"Cynthia" says Brooke, "if I didn't know better I would swear you were going crazy, but I get your point." Gathering her handbag, brochures, cell phone and maps from the large table in the middle of the room, "let's go Joyce, I don't know about you but I know when I'm not wanted. At least right now, I am very happy I am not wanted."

Joyce winks at Cynthia, "smart girl, now let's get out of here."

Picking up her overnight bag and making her way toward the door, Joyce stops to look back at Cynthia. "Just promise me you will get that sweater finished. It's been so long I can't even remember what it's supposed to look like. Enjoy your time and I will see you when you get home."

"Trust me, I will call you as soon as I finish it and when I get home you will be the first to see it," says Cynthia.

"Enjoy dear friend."

"Have a good flight Joyce. Call me later so I know you arrived safely."

"Cynthia" calls out Brooke, "if you need me for any reason - any reason at all, call me. I'll have my cell phone with me and I will make sure Brad and I don't go too far outside the city. Promise you'll call if you need me?"

"I promise. Just have a good time, you deserve it. I'll see you later."

As she closes the door after them and turns slowly heading toward the oversized Queen Anne chair, "Now what do I do?"

Chapter Fourteen

Getting up from her comfortable chair, 'it never fails, just when you find that good comfortable spot and settle in the phone rings. Okay, what did you forget?"

"Excuse me? Cynthia it's Rusty did I catch you at a bad time?"

"Oh Rusty I am so sorry," sounding like a nine year old caught taking ice cream from the freezer. "I thought it was Joyce calling because she forgot something. She left for the airport twenty minutes ago."

"I know I had a chance to say goodbye when I saw them in the lobby. Joyce told me you were still here. I really am sorry if I disturbed you."

"Please don't apologize you are not disturbing me. I was just sitting here trying to figure out what I would do with this day. I can't remember the last time I had nothing on my agenda pulling me in fifty different directions so, before I call the office I thought I would take a few minutes to see how normal people live."

"And what conclusion did you come up with?"

"Well for openers, I don't know what normal is and really can't define it. Also, that my life has been so focused and planned for so long, I am totally lost when there is nothing on my calendar. And now for the big revelation – I don't do well with free time. You can start laughing."

"Well I really don't see anything to laugh about or anything unusual. You fall right in line with approximately 98% of the people I work with and deal with on a regular basis myself included. The only difference, my revelation about free time came a lot sooner than yours and since that time I make sure I do something strictly for me when I can. In other words, I have learned to enjoy a life outside of work and I love it. I made myself a promise that I would never look back or revert back to a life that only included work. That's one of the reasons I enjoy the time with my Mom and our dancing. After my Dad died she was totally lost. But somehow she figured out what her life should be without him and she has perfected the ability to carve out time for herself that focuses solely on what she wants to do. Her philosophy certainly changed my life and my sister's. I'm sorry I didn't mean to ramble on like this. I'll let you get back to enjoying your free time, but the main purpose for my call is to apologize to you."

"Apologize to me?" answers a surprised Cynthia. "Why do you need to apologize to me?"

"Well, last night I was way out of line when I reached for your hand. I'm not sorry I did, but it was wrong. For a brief moment I totally forgot that all of us had just met. I'll chalk it up to the 'one for all, all for one hand clasp moment' we had last night at Café Du Monde. It has been a long time since I've felt so comfortable with anyone and the thought that all of us were strangers just hours before we met at Café Firebird never came to mind. I just needed you to know that. Please enjoy the rest of your day and I hope your merger gets back on track very soon. Take care."

"Wait," she calls out realizing she doesn't want him to hang up. "Don't I get a chance to say something?"

"I'm sorry. Sure you do."

"Well, thank you for that. Look, there is no need to apologize a friendly gesture never needs an apology."

"I appreciate your kindness Cynthia, but it wasn't just.........uh, okay, thank you."

"Again, no apology needed. You know Mr. Tate, for an attorney you certainly seem to be at a loss for words today."

"Ouch!" unable to hold back the laughter.

"No seriously," says Cynthia, "last night was a wonderful mix of good food, good music, great dancing, good friendships and loads of laughter. No one should apologize for that. But, I'll tell you what - to make sure you don't continue to feel as though you owe me an apology how about buying me lunch? Maybe this is a good time to explore that family tree. In all these years I've never met anyone else named Tate."

Stammering and a little stunned by her suggestion, "I would be honored."

"Great, it's 11:45 now so why don't we meet in the lobby at 12:30 and we can decide at that time where we will go for lunch oh, and just one more thing – no beignets," sounding more upbeat than she should. "I love them but I've had more than enough to last me on this trip. Okay with you?"

Sounding like a high school junior just finding out he has a date for the Junior Prom, "deal, Cynthia Farrell. I will meet you in the lobby at 12:30."

Placing the phone back on its base, she pauses, stunned by what she has just said and done. Turning back toward the Queen Anne chair, she sinks into it. "Oh my stars what have I done. I just steam rolled a total stranger into buying me lunch. This is not me! I've never done anything like this in my life. Why him? What made me agree to spend time with him today? That's it! I am going to call him back and tell him something came up and I can't make it." Getting up from the chair she heads toward the phone. As she aims her hand toward the receiver, that pesky voice inside her head speaks up once again – *'wait a minute, why cancel. He's a fun guy and everyone had a good time last night, why not go to lunch with him? Why lie to him? Is that to make him feel better or yourself? So he squeezed your hand and held you close to him on the dance floor. It's only lunch Cynthia, and you are curious about his Tate family. What's the big deal?'* Now, stopping dead in her tracks in front of the phone, she withdraws her hand - "you're right," answering back to the pesky voice, "it is only lunch. He is a nice guy. What the heck is wrong with that?" Remembering Joyce's comment – "last night something happened, I don't know what but from where I was sitting something did. I'm not here to determine right or wrong but whatever it is, if it makes you happy – even for a little while, you truly deserve it." As she steps away from the phone she realizes just what Joyce's words mean. "Yes, I did feel something when he held me on the dance floor and when he squeezed my hand - but what? Why?" With the realization that now is as good a time as any to find an answer to that why – she reaches for her purse and camera on the hall table, checks to make sure she has her key and heads out the door.

Chapter Fifteen

Stepping out of the elevator she sees Rusty talking to Franklin at the Concierge Desk. As she approaches, "okay you two what are you cooking up?" Franklin turning toward her, "good afternoon Mrs. Farrell. I had hoped I would get a chance to see you on this trip. It was such a delight meeting your assistant Brooke. I hope we didn't overwhelm her with things to do?"

"You probably did but it was all good. This is her first trip to New Orleans and I promised her she would have an opportunity to see as much as we could squeeze in. You made that much easier for me Franklin, thank you."

"No thanks necessary, Mrs. Farrell. That's what I'm here for. In fact, Mr. Tate and I were discussing various things to put on his agenda for the day. Let me introduce you."

Now looking directly at Rusty and into those gorgeous eyes, "thank you Franklin but we met last night, however I would like to listen to your suggestions as to what sight-seeing adventure you have in mind," trying not to let on that she would be spending the day with him.

"Actually Mrs. Farrell, I could very easily lose my job to Mr. Tate. His knowledge of New Orleans history and culture is astounding. In fact, very few people outside of New Orleans are aware of the Creole Cottages and Shotguns history that played such an important role in the shaping of this city. I thought they were all torn down but Mr. Tate just reminded me that several are still very much intact."

Glancing toward Rusty with a slight smile, "well I'm impressed."

"Don't be. That knowledge might just win a prize for me on a game show, but little else."

"I wouldn't buy that if I were you Mrs. Farrell," says Franklin. "Mr. Tate is being much too modest about his extensive knowledge of New Orleans history. Every time he is here I am reminded a little more about those things that most of us who were born and raised here have forgotten."

"Okay, that's enough. I just might begin to believe all of this good stuff you are saying about me. Franklin, thank you and let's try to have lunch again before I leave, like we did last month."

"I would be delighted. Let me know your schedule and I will make sure I'm available. Enjoy your day Mr. Tate and you also Mrs. Farrell. I'm sure Brooke is eager to get started. I haven't seen her yet."

"Oh, Brooke took a good friend of mine to the airport early this morning. Today I'm kind of on my own," she says sheepishly hoping she doesn't raise any questions in his mind.

"Well enjoy no matter what direction you head in," says Franklin. "Perhaps Mr. Tate will share his knowledge of the area with you."

As Franklin finished that sentence their eyes locked. Cynthia couldn't help wondering what he was thinking, especially since he felt the need to apologize to her for reaching out for her hand last night. Now, beginning to feel this idea of lunch and spending the day together was a huge mistake, she wanted to tell him she would not join him. But for some unexplainable reason she couldn't bring herself to say it. The thought of not spending the day with him made her sad and she couldn't explain why! As they gazed into each other's eyes, neither one realized that Franklin was no longer a part of the group. Now feeling very uncomfortable, she knew this would be the perfect time to tell him she would not join him. "Uh Rusty, I think it would be a good idea if...."

"Mrs. Farrell, hello, Mrs. Farrell." Startled out of her uneasy feeling by the sound of someone calling her name, she glances around the lobby. Looking toward the front desk she sees Margie waving to her, motioning to her to come to the desk. Thankful for the opportunity to not stare into his eyes and a halt to her uneasiness, "Oh Rusty, please excuse me Margie is calling to me. I'll be right back."

Approaching the front desk, "Hi Margie, is everything okay?"

"Mrs. Farrell I'm glad I caught you before you left," calls out Margie. "I have a message for you from Mr. Benedict. He would like for you to give him a call as soon as you can. He said he tried calling your room a couple of times then called me to see if you were lunching in the hotel. He said to reach him at the office."

"Thank you very much Margie, I'll give him a call now." As she makes her way back toward Rusty, with cell phone in hand, "I'm sorry but I need to return a call to my boss."

"Please don't apologize," says a concerned Rusty and sounding a little disappointed believing the day will now change. "I'll wait for you outside. I had the garage bring my car around."

"Hi Jason, what's going on?"

"Everything is okay, Cyn. Hoban will return on Sunday and the three of us will have dinner at 8:00 in the Executive Dining Room. Everyone will be back in town so signing can take place early Monday morning. Right now, we've scheduled the meeting for 10:00 a.m. There will be a luncheon immediately followed by a press conference and it's all over. Well, that part is over. The real work for us will just begin as we setup meetings with employees of the new company to brief them of the changes. But we can discuss that when I get there. I should be at the hotel around 2:30 on Sunday. I don't see a need to head back before Sunday, especially since you are still there. You can certainly take care of anything that comes up but I doubt if anything will. So relax, enjoy the next couple of days. You've earned them. I hope Brad delivered my message as intended?"

"Oh, he delivered it alright. I especially enjoyed the 'firing' part."

Laughing, "good for him, I'll see you Sunday. Enjoy!"

"Yes sir! In fact, I was practically out the door to go wandering. It's been a very long time since I was presented with a couple of days just for me."

"Well make the most of them now, I'm not sure when either one of us will see them again during the next year. See you Sunday."

"See you Sunday, have a safe trip." Slipping her cell phone back into its case and into her shoulder bag, she is puzzled by her feeling of total relief. So much so that she is glad she did not end this day with Rusty. Now, more than ever she is looking forward to it. For the first time in many years, the realization that she cannot control everything around her doesn't frighten her at all. Remembering something her Mother told her just before illness changed her forever. "My darling Cynthia, I can't get over just how much you have become like me but please, don't adopt my life. I truly believed I controlled everything. To make everything fit the way I wanted it to fit I had to do it, I had to make it happen. Then one day I woke up and realized I didn't control anything. You have to educate yourself and learn skills to adapt to changing circumstances. We like to believe we control our lives and everything in it, but we don't. Live for today Cynthia and, if we prepare ourselves the right way, when tomorrow gets here we won't have any trouble knowing how to proceed."

As she makes her way toward the front door, she is totally lost in remembering her Mother's words 'live for today Cynthia, worry about tomorrow, tomorrow.'

"Uh, excuse me, is everything okay?"

Shaken from her thoughts she stops a few feet from the voice. As she turns around she is embarrassed seeing Rusty standing by his car realizing she just walked passed him.

"Is everything all right?" he questions.

"Rusty I am so sorry. Talk about getting lost in your thoughts. I guess I just proved what that means. Please, please don't take it personally. Let's just chalk it up to now having the next four days just for me. I don't think I even know what that feels like."

"Well I hope you are up to finding out," says Rusty. "I can tell you from personal experience, when I first found myself in that kind of situation, I didn't know what to do. In fact I spent three days of the five I had facing me going over papers in my briefcase that I had already gone over days before I got on the plane to come here for a major meeting. That meeting was delayed, like yours, and I was totally lost."

"Well from where I stand," says a surprised Cynthia, "it looks as though you learned very quickly how to get over it."

"To be perfectly honest I didn't do so well in the beginning. But it didn't take long for me to find ways to do things just for me and I have never looked back. This is an amazing world we live in Cynthia. This city is amazing. If having a couple of days for yourself, unplanned, unexpected is new for you, don't look back. Just make the most of them and I can assure you, you will never be sorry you did."

"Well, Mr. Tate. That sounds like a good philosophy to me. So what does this day have in store for us?"

"After speaking with Franklin and if you are not familiar with the history, I thought it might be a good idea to tour a Creole Cottage/Shotgun neighborhood and stop by one of my favorite places, The Beauregard-Keyes House. How does that sound?"

"Lead the way. I'm in no position to say no since all I ever see when I am in town is the hotel lobby, my suite and Café Du Monde. You have my permission to educate me."

Looking directly into her eyes and feeling a lot less apologetic for reaching for her hand last night "it will be my pleasure," reaching his hand out to hers to help her into the car.

As Cynthia gently places her hand in his there is a sense of being cared for and feeling special – very special. A feeling that has all but died during the last few years as both she and Art 'climbed' the ladders of success. A feeling she didn't believe was necessary, until now. A feeling that should disturb her because the man gently, yet firmly holding her hand, is not her husband. A feeling so comforting she doesn't want to let it get away. As Rusty settles himself in the driver's seat and pulls away from the curb she can hear her Mother's voice in her head – *'live for today. You won't know what tomorrow brings until tomorrow gets here. You can't control it – live for today!'*

Chapter Sixteen

As Rusty aims the car toward the curb in front of several row houses, each one revealing more architectural splendor than the next, Cynthia is amazed at what stands before her. Each house more beautiful than the one next to it with stately designed windows, some painted beautiful soft shades of yellow with green shutters, some with crude looking clapboard panels showing how parts of yesterday can be preserved with caring. "Rusty is this what you call Creole Cottage and Shotgun?" exclaims a surprised Cynthia.

"It certainly is. What do you think?"

"I can't believe the years I've traveled to this city and never even knew these homes existed. Is it possible to go inside?"

"Absolutely and I can't believe we found a parking space this close, usually I am several blocks away. You must be bringing me good luck."

"I doubt that, but thanks for the thought." Changing the subject very quickly, "I can't wait to see what the interiors look like. How did you ever discover these?"

"I have my Dad to thank for this one. Growing up my sister and I loved his stories about New Orleans history. He went to law school here, so every school vacation and holiday Vivian and I begged him to bring us here so we could see it for ourselves. Some parents take their kids fishing or send them off to summer camp, my parents gave us a sense of yesterday not only here in New Orleans, but New York, North Carolina, Chicago, Colorado, Utah. I could go on forever the list is so long. So a couple of times a year and especially during summer vacation, we packed tons of stuff in our old 1973 Chevy and hit the road. My parents were like two teenagers hunting for buried treasure in any state the spirit moved them to head toward, and Vivian and I lapped it up like two thirsty cubs." Realizing how he must sound, "man I can't believe I am boring you with this story." Quickly changing the subject, "I'm glad we found this parking space. This gives us an opportunity to walk through each of the houses so you can get a sense of what life was like back then."

"No you're not boring me, please tell me more," practically shouting at him. "I'm beginning to feel my early education was sorely lacking since we never traveled much. With one sister and five brothers my Dad's life was all work. Travel for us meant an occasional car ride to visit relatives in Connecticut and I can count on one hand, with many fingers left over, how often we did that. Please, I'm curious why they are called Creole and Shotgun," -- all the time thinking *'what I really want is to hold on to this moment alone with you.'*

Turning off the motor he swings around toward her. *Looking directly at her he couldn't help but think about how he felt when he raised his hand to give her back the ball of yarn that rolled out of her bag during the security check at Newark Airport. She is so beautiful he thought to himself - elegant, charming, poised, smart and very beautiful. When her fingers lightly touched mine as she reached for the yarn, I knew I had to know more about her. Now fate has placed her here, so close, hanging on to each word as I talk about New Orleans history and I can't take my eyes off of her.*

Not realizing he is staring at her "h-e-l-l-o. Rusty – hello is anyone in there," waving her hand in front of his face. "Wow, and I thought I was the only one who totally zoned out on occasion," chuckles Cynthia. "Are you okay, am I boring you with my many questions?"

Slightly startled by her voice and now feeling extremely embarrassed – "I am so sorry" he stammers.

"I'm sorry," she says. "Sometimes my sense of humor leaves a lot to be desired. We don't have to sit here if you don't want to," as she reaches for the car door. "It's just that I was so taken with your knowledge of this place and feeling really cheated that I did not have the kind of experience growing up that you and your sister shared."

"Cynthia, I am sorry. Please, I will be more than happy to fill you in about the history."

Feeling more at ease as they sit close together, "I'm not sure where to start but here goes – keep in mind this is my Dad's version but he wasn't too far off the mark."

As she continues to stare into those glorious pale brown eyes waiting for him to tell her more about this amazing city, she thinks back to

Newark Airport and her fingers touching the softness of his hand as she retrieved her yarn and now, the thought of those hands holding her, touching her, *'what the heck is wrong with me? Why do I feel this way?' As he starts his story, she is struck by the fact that she doesn't care why she feels the way she does. Settling into her seat as she shifts her body to look directly at him – this is my today.*

Chapter Seventeen

"Wow what an amazing tour and history," exclaims Cynthia as they head toward the car. "I can't wait to tell my girls and bring them here, they will be fascinated to know that in the 1800's Creole Cottages and Shotguns were the homes of the working class, free blacks and immigrants and since they were inexpensive to build and were on small lots, it made them affordable to everyone who dreamed of owning their own home. Did I get it right?"

"By George, I think she's got it," he says chuckling.

"You're real funny Mr. Tate, and I was always under the impression lawyers did not have much of a sense of humor."

"Double ouch!"

"Just kidding and please don't take it personally, remember I'm married to an attorney. One more question, who originally designed these homes?"

"The Creole Cottage was designed by Jean-Louis Dolliole, a prominent builder and a free person of color. Also, this Shotgun was once home to Armand Piron, a jazz musician who taught music lessons from the front parlor. The Creole Cottage is an architectural style common in the Caribbean easy to build and inexpensive. I don't know if you noticed but the casement windows are a major part of the design because they can be shuttered to block noise or opened to allow light. That's what made them a perfect design for this area."

"You know, what surprised me most is that the Cottages were only two rooms wide and two rooms deep and the Shotgun had four rooms," says Cynthia. "I love the name Shotgun and that it came from the idea that a bullet could travel unimpeded from the front through the back of the house. Okay," says Cynthia, "what's next on my historical tour?"

"Well considering it is almost 4:30 we can grab a late lunch or have an early dinner. It's your call."

Glancing at her watch, "my stars I had no idea it was that late. I also can't believe my stomach didn't signal me to eat at 1:30. Every day I can tell what time it is without looking at my watch just listening to my stomach. I guess there is something to be said for time flying when you're having fun."

Staring at her and surprised by her comment as they stand by the car, "well thank you, I am extremely pleased to hear you are having fun, I know I am."

Returning his gaze, "to be honest with you I can't remember the last time I have so thoroughly enjoyed an afternoon – with or without lunch."

"Well on that note," he responds casually hoping to ease some of the tension he is feeling standing so close to her, "let's eat."

"Another good suggestion for the day Mr. Tate, but nothing fancy."

"Okay, what do you feel like eating and where should we go?"

"Well it is very clear to me that you know this city much better than I do, so I am more than happy to leave the choice up to you."

"Let me think, well two of my favorites are not too far from here. Joey K's is located in a wood–framed corner building with a gallery wrapping around the second floor. The dining room is usually filled with locals looking for good food and they know the prices are fair. On the other end of the spectrum is Nat and Maddie's Restaurant, more on the gourmet meal side. The owner/chef prides himself on traditional Louisiana dishes and the fact that all of the ingredients are local and guaranteed super fresh. Take your pick."

"If memory serves me correctly, I do recall I'm leaving the decisions up to you."

"Okay, but I don't want to hear about this later in the event you are not completely happy, deal?"

"You've got yourself a deal, Mr. Tate!"

"Then off to Nat and Maddie's we go," responds an enthusiastic Rusty.

"Lead and I shall follow," answers Cynthia.

Easing his hand toward her elbow to assist her into the car, he is suddenly aware of the fact that this could be the last time he sees her. Right now the only thing he knows for sure is that he doesn't want that to happen. He wants to spend time with her. He needs to spend time with her. As she slips into her seat, "Cynthia I just had a great idea."

Looking up at him as he leans against the car, she couldn't help but wonder *is he married or involved with someone. Anyone as handsome, intellectually gifted, friendly and fun to be with surely must have someone in his life. Why would he even want to spend time with me? More importantly - why do I care?*

"Cynthia, did you hear me?"

Startled by the sound of his voice although staring directly at him, "what, oh, I'm sorry, what did you say?"

"Now who is zoning out?" he asks smiling.

"Watch it Mr. Tate, you're skating on thin ice," smiling back at him.

"I said I had a great idea."

"Well get in the car and tell me your great idea."

As he gently closes the door and walks around the front of the car she can't take her eyes off of him and thinking - *he moves with such a sense of who he is. Remembering how firmly and close he held her last night, how easily she slipped into his arms, how comfortable and at ease she felt there and his confidence as he lead her around the dance floor.* Shutting her eyes to relive that moment, she is startled by the sound of the car door closing. Feeling silly and a little ashamed she aims her gaze out the front window not wanting to give the slightest clue that her thoughts are centered on him and those thoughts might reveal what she is feeling. Feelings that should end this day right now, but she doesn't want it to end. *Why, she thinks, why him, why now, why?*

"Cynthia, are you okay?"

"What, oh, I'm fine. Why do you ask?"

"Well, you had your eyes closed. I'm afraid I tired you with my stories and sightseeing so if you want to change your mind about dinner I'll understand," sounding disappointed.

"You know Rusty that might not be such a bad idea. The last two days have been a little unsettling and I guess I'm beginning to feel it now. I'm sorry." *As she listens to her words, she knows there is no truth to them. The only unsettling thing about last night and today are her unexplainable feelings for him and running from those feelings makes a lot of sense right now.*

"No, please don't apologize, I understand." As he starts the car he is hit with the thought that this is it. Except for, maybe, an occasional passing by in the lobby or another dropped ball of yarn, he will probably never see her again.

Driving along not speaking their silence is shattered when Cynthia remembers he said he had a great idea.

Turning toward him, "Rusty, I recall you mentioning you had a great idea, but you never said what it was."

"Oh, don't worry about that. It will keep."

"No come on, tell me. Ideas come and go – very rarely do I hear great ones. Tell me."

"Well, I had this bright idea about sharing other insights about New Orleans with you. I thought maybe we could do this again, another day. I got the impression there is so much about New Orleans that you don't know or haven't seen that, perhaps, well, that's okay."

"Hmm, let me think about it. It does sound like a good idea. I have three more days I can call my own. What does your schedule look like for the next couple of days? I could learn more about New Orleans and we haven't explored the family tree yet. Although, what you told me about your Dad and what I know about mine, I doubt if they were even remotely related. What did you have in mind?" surprised at hearing herself ask the question. But for some unexplainable reason, she didn't care. The only thing she knew for sure is that she did not want to let him slip away from her - at least not now.

"My business schedule wraps tomorrow around 6 o'clock and I scheduled a couple of days off to enjoy what I enjoy about this city before I leave on Sunday."

Without hesitating, although she knew she should, "well, that sounds like a plan to me. Start planning and we can touch base tomorrow night to set up a time to meet Thursday evening or Friday. You decide on what you think I should see I couldn't even begin to suggest anything. As I mentioned to you before, when I am in town my New Orleans is very limited. What a novel idea for me to actually get to know the city I spend at least one-quarter of my business life in. Wait there is one thing I would really like to see, 'The City of the Dead'. Ever since I was little I have been fascinated by the pictures of the tombs and the thought that everyone is buried above ground. It would be great to finally see it up close. Can we work that in?"

"Consider it worked," he says with such enthusiasm you would think he just learned he hit a million dollar lottery. "It's a date, uh I mean, it's a good jumping off place to start seeing the real New Orleans."

Amused by his choice of the word date, but not offended, "well whatever it is I look forward to it and I will check with Brooke to see what she wants to do. I......her statement is halted by the sound of her cell phone. "Excuse me Rusty, I totally forgot I had it with me and I can't believe this is the first time it has gone off. Just imagine what life was like before this invention. Hello, Arthur, hi – how is everything?" she says with hesitation. The sound of his voice bringing her back into a world that, for a very brief moment, she didn't even think about.

"Are the girls okay? Good. How was your meeting with the Governor? What do you mean at least he didn't fire you? They know better. They know they've got the best of the best."

As Rusty eases up to the hotel, he is struck by the sound of her voice – casual, carefree, not at all like the apprehensive, questioning business executive he spent the day with. Listening to the 'laughter' in her voice, glancing toward her catching a brief glimpse at the loving, playful expression on her face, he realizes she is more beautiful than when he first saw her at Newark Airport. Although trying hard to ignore the conversation with her husband, he can't help feeling jealous that he isn't the one on the other end of the phone. As he listens to her conversation it's not guilt he feels about eaves dropping and his feelings, but a sense of loss and disappointment he will not have her all to himself if Brooke joins them on Thursday or Friday and, for this brief moment they are still together, he has to share her with her husband. *'How stupid,' he thinks to himself. 'She obviously has shared a good life with this man. Who am I to sit here feeling jealous? Why do I feel jealous?' Sitting next to her thinking about his feelings he knows the questions in his head, right now, have no answers.*

"I'm really glad for you Art. It was about time the Governor and the Mayor saw things your way – or I should say, got out of your way. Congratulations. By the way, suppose I told you that I just spent the afternoon with a very charming and handsome young man. What – what do you mean - right? Do you really think I would make something like that up? You know what I'll have my picture taken with him to show you he is real. No, he is not a model, he is not an actor, and….forget it, think whatever you like. Right now I'm on my way to dinner, so I will get back to you when I return to the hotel. You take care. Bye."

"So you think I'm charming and handsome," says Rusty with a wide grin.

Now feeling extremely embarrassed, "I'm sorry, I should have just told him I would call him back. I didn't mean to make you feel uncomfortable."

"No, I wasn't uncomfortable I truly appreciate the compliment. The things that most people say about me, that I know of, don't even come close to your comments."

"I find that hard to believe but, you know what, let's just change the subject," feeling like a thirteen year old who just revealed she has a crush on a classmate. "Tell you what."

"What," answers Rusty totally interested in what she has in mind.

"If it's not too far from here, let's head to Nat and Maddie's. I realize we are just a few feet from the hotel but suddenly I'm feeling the need for a good dinner right now."

"Your wish is my command and no, it's not too far," as they pass the hotel.

Chapter Eighteen

"Well Ms. Brooke, do you think you've seen enough of New Orleans to last you until you get back here again?" quizzes Brad.

"Are you kidding" she shoots back, "I could not have dreamed up this day to make it any better. I really can't begin to thank you enough. I feel like I've just had the history lesson of a life time."

"Today was just the beginning. Believe me there is tons more I would like to show you. Please don't thank me it's been a long time since I've had this much fun and the time to indulge myself in wandering around New Orleans. Besides, I'm still on contract to Mr. Benedict and one of the last things he said to me when I dropped him off at the airport Tuesday night was to make sure you and Mrs. Farrell, I mean Cynthia, get to see everything you want to because both of you have been working really hard on this project."

"Are you kidding me? Did he really include me along with Cynthia? Most of the time I think he doesn't even know I'm alive until he needs something from a file in her office."

"Oh, don't underestimate him Brooke. He is very much aware of your existence and what contributions you've made to the running of Cynthia's office. I know it seems as though he only thinks and talks business, but he is very much a down-to-earth kind of guy and very knowledgeable about everything. He said you are very smart, funny and, if it wasn't for Cynthia, he would steal you away to run his office."

"No way, you aren't just saying that to make me feel good, are you?"

"I've gotten to know Mr. Benedict very well over the last eighteen months I've been assigned to him. In the beginning it was touch and go but then he started asking for me each time he came to town. After that, the dispatcher permanently assigned me as his driver. I don't believe he would say those things just for my benefit if he really didn't mean them."

"You know Brad, Cynthia also mentioned to me on the flight down that he liked me and I wasn't sure I should believe her. I thought she was just saying it to make me......"

"Hey, relax. You are a dedicated worker and a true asset to that company and both Jason and Cynthia know it. Just accept it for what it is."

"And what is it?"

"That you are a dedicated worker and a true asset to the company," smiling as he looks directly at her.

Now doubled over with laughter, "you are a real piece of work Brad."

Laughing, "thank you, I'll take that as a compliment. So, should we stop and get something to eat or are you ready to call it a day? I've shown you the day time New Orleans, are you up for seeing a little of the night time New Orleans?" Brad asks.

"You mean there's a difference."

"Oh my dear Ms. Stephenson, you have not truly lived until you have experienced New Orleans night life," he answers.

"Well to be perfectly honest, I'm not a night life type of girl and since we had very little to eat after Joyce's plane took off I could really go for a good dinner."

"Oh man, now I'm beginning to feel guilty not having fed you throughout the day. You should have said something. I've been so focused on making sure you go back to New Jersey with a true feeling of New Orleans."

"Hey, I'm a big girl. I could have yelled feed me. The time went by so quickly and we were having so much fun, it just never occurred to me to eat too. However, right now I am starving."

"Say no more. Tell me what you feel like eating and we are on our way."

"Hey this is your town and my first time. I wouldn't even begin to know where to start. It's on you pal."

"Okay," replies a very pleased Brad knowing he gets to spend a few more hours with her. "It is now 6:30, we can either go back to the hotel, the dining room there is terrific, or the Cabaret Club again. Or...."

"They both would be okay but what about something that is very New Orleans, maybe even away from the French Quarter and into one of the regular neighborhoods. How does that sound?"

"That sounds pretty good to me. Let me find a parking space and we can look at some of the flyers I have in the trunk of the car. I don't want the responsibility of deciding on something and you might not like it. We'll do this together. What do you think?"

"Get to parking before I starve to death," looking directly into his eyes and thinking, *'no one has ever been this nice to me except Cynthia.'*

"Yes ma'am, you don't have to tell me twice," as he aims his block long limo toward an available space.

As the car comes to a stop and he reaches for the door - *'why couldn't he live in New Jersey? After this trip I will never see him again and I have never felt so comfortable and safe with anyone else in my entire life. I wish this day, no this trip would never end.'* As Brad settles himself back behind the wheel he is holding a huge stack of outlandishly colored brochures and flyers.

"You've got to be kidding! All of those brochures just to find one restaurant?"

"My dear Ms. Brooke, you are in New Orleans now. Sit back and feast your eyes on information detailing the best eats in town. Let's see."

As he thumbs through the stack tossing aside some and dropping in her lap others, she tells herself before she gets on that plane and heads back to New Jersey she has to find out if there is someone in his life. *He may not be interested, she thinks to herself, but I'm not going to leave here without finding out.*

"Hey," he calls forcing her thoughts back to the business of the moment. "Look through the brochures and flyers I just dropped in your lap and let me know if anything interests you. I don't have a preference so I'll leave it up to you."

"No way, I wouldn't even know where to begin. I like just about any kind of food, although I've never tasted real Cajun cooking. If you are ever in New Jersey or New York then I'll do the picking. Here, it's your call fella."

"Okay, but remember if you don't like my choice it's your own fault."

"Oh, I'll like it," she says with an obvious double meaning.

As Brad turns to look at her, he smiles with as much of a double meaning as her comment about what and where they will eat. "Well, if that's the case I think I know the perfect place that will also add to the history of New Orleans you picked up today."

"Wow, that's sounds intriguing. What do you have in mind?"

"Well, one of my favorite places is Arnaud's and I haven't been there in ages. Also, I think you would love it. If we do eat there, after dinner we can go up to the second floor to see a collection of Carnival gowns and other memorabilia in the Germaine Wells Mardi Gras Museum. Arnaud's has been here since 1918 and their specialty is Creole cuisine and the very best is Shrimp Arnaud and Oysters Bienville. My parents met there, married soon after and for as long as I can remember my brother and I were dragged there every anniversary, birthday and the day they met."

"Wait, I thought you said it was one of your favorites."

"Well, it is and has been for the past 13 years. But when you are 8, 12, 15, etc. and you would prefer to have franks and beans or a hamburger, you really don't appreciate that kind of food. As an adult, it's a different story. I try to get there every chance I can but, unfortunately, that doesn't happen often enough. Should we go?" *As she sits quietly she can't help thinking – 'does he have a special person he takes there or.....'*

"Brooke did you hear me? I asked if that sounds like something you want to do."

"Oh gosh, I'm sorry. I guess I was so focused on hearing about the food my mind drifted off. Yes, yes, it sounds like a great place plus I love fashion. The opportunity to see a collection of authentic Carnival gowns and New Orleans history sounds great. Let's go."

"Great. Oh, I forgot to mention, Arnaud's also has live traditional jazz. So just in case there isn't another opportunity before you leave, you will have soaked up some traditional New Orleans jazz culture. "But" as he starts the car, "if there is another opportunity to share my city with you, I've got a list of places to go, people to see, things to do and food to try. The Palm Court Jazz Café inside an antique French Market warehouse is where we'll go for jambalaya and crawfish pie. You can't leave New Orleans without tasting jambalaya and crawfish pie."

Watching his lips move she is touched by the excitement on his face as he talks about sharing his city with her, even though she has no idea what jambalaya and crawfish pie is and afraid of sounding stupid if she asks. "Brad, I really can't thank you enough for the time you spent with me today. I've seen more during the past few hours than I thought I would ever see the entire time I'm here."

"Hey, you sound as though this is the end of the tour. I know Mr. Benedict will not return until Sunday, so......oh wait, I almost forgot – Cynthia. I know she wanted to show you New Orleans and here I go making plans to drag you all over town. I'm sorry."

"No, don't apologize. If I know Cynthia she was probably pleased to have this day to herself. I know she promised to show me around but I am sure having this time to just relax and finish her daughter's sweater was probably like a little slice of heaven for her. She works so hard and is so dedicated to everything she does – the company and everyone in it, her husband and daughters, I sometimes wonder when she ever takes time to do something for herself.   Actually Brad, if you don't mind showing me more of New Orleans, then Cynthia will have the time to relax and do just what she wants to. She'll probably put up a fuss but I think I can convince her to take advantage of the fact that this free time landed in our laps and that she can have this time just for herself." Suddenly feeling embarrassed and ashamed that she sounds like she is forcing herself on him, "I mean, if you don't mind."

"If you are sure it will be okay with Cynthia, it is definitely okay with me. I would hate to have Mr. Benedict think I neglected my responsibilities in looking out for the two of you and being available to you – I mean to you both."

With a slight smile, "I'm sure Cynthia won't mind. So while we wait for our dinner to arrive let's look over that stack of brochures and flyers you have and see where we will point this car during the next couple of days. Once everyone returns on Sunday, it's all over and back to business as usual."

"Sounds like a plan to me."

"Brad, it sounds like a very good plan to me, drive on sir."

As he eases the car from its parked space, "Ma lady, your wish is my command."

"Wow," says Brooke, "I could adjust to this kind of life very easily."

Chapter Nineteen

"Hey," whispers Brooke as she quietly makes her way toward Cynthia sitting at the large round dining table in their suite. "How was your day yesterday? I hope I didn't disturb you too much by getting in kind of late last night. After we left the airport, Brad mentioned a couple of places he would like to show me then before we knew it, it was time to get dinner, then we......"

"It's okay, slow down. Obviously you had a fabulous time," teases Cynthia, totally amused by the excitement of this young adult sounding as though she just sat on Santa's lap for the first time in her life, to tell him everything she wanted for Christmas.

"I'm sorry, yesterday was so unbelievable I don't think I will ever have both feet on the ground again."

"Whoa" calls out Cynthia with a slight smile, "it's not over yet. We still have three more days we can call our own unless Brad showed you everything this wonderful place has to offer."

"Are you kidding," she says as she sits at the table across from Cynthia. "I don't think I could see everything New Orleans has to offer even if I stayed here for a year."

"Okay, let's order breakfast in and you can tell me everything you did yesterday and I will tell you how I spent my day."

"Oh I think I can answer that right now," shoots back Brooke.

"Oh really," answers a quizzical Cynthia. "This I've got to hear. But hold onto that thought until we order. What would you like for breakfast," as she reaches for the phone to call Room Service.

"I'm almost too excited to eat," says Brooke.

"Well that's a first" responds a very surprised Cynthia, "I remember when you had the flu a couple of months ago with a fever of 103, aching everywhere and still managed to gobble up in less than five minutes the food I brought to you. Everyone else I know, including myself, would not have eaten anything at all for days, but not you. Now you want me to believe that you are too excited to eat. I can't wait to hear what your day was like. Come on, let's order and then I want all of the details while we wait for it to get here. Plus, we should plan what we will do with this day."

"All right, if you say so. I'll have a large orange juice, mushroom and spinach omelet with cornbread muffins and a dish of cinnamon apples, a pot of tea and a large glass of iced water."

Laughing so hard she didn't hear the voice on the other end answer – "Room Service, how may I help you Mrs. Farrell."

"I am so sorry I didn't hear you at first, good morning. I'll have two large orange juice, two spinach and mushroom omelets, cornbread muffins, cinnamon apples, a large pot of tea and pitcher of iced water, please."

"Thank you Mrs. Farrell. We will have that up to you in ten minutes."

"Thank you." As Cynthia places the phone back on the cradle, she sits staring across the table at Brooke.

"What what," calls out Brooke "what's with the stare? Have I grown another head or something? What?"

"Okay Ms. Stephenson, our food will arrive in approximately ten minutes. I want details of everything you did from the time you left this hotel to take Joyce to the airport to the time you put your key in this door. Don't leave anything out. I get the feeling this is going to be good."

"Cynthia, you must be kidding. I don't think I can remember everything - there was so much that…."

"When I say details I mean details so don't even try to change the subject. There is no way I am going to believe you spent the day with a very nice, attractive young man, seeing sights around New Orleans, getting in late last night and now this morning claiming you are too excited to eat, and not fill me in," she says smiling.

"See, I did disturb you last night."

"You didn't disturb me. I never heard you come in – in fact I believe you got in before me."

"WHAT!" shouts Brooke, "now who has details to share? Are you telling me that you did not stay here all day working on Jean's sweater?"

"I certainly did not," replies a very coy Cynthia.

"Oh brother - you told Joyce you were going to stay in and work on that sweater. Didn't you?"

"Well, it started out that way. But – hey, wait a minute, I don't have to explain my day to you," she says with a grin as wide as a slice of watermelon.

"You sly little fox you. This is going to be good."

"Uh, excuse me but weren't you the one who talked about stepping into a fantasy life?"

"Yeah" she says hesitantly, "but that was about me."

"Well if I remember that conversation correctly, I indicated that a little fantasy might be good for me also."

"You know what! You look like my boss, but I'm not sure you sound like my boss so start explaining. What happened to change your mind about finishing that sweater?"

"Well"

[Knock-knock]

"Oh, look at that – breakfast is here," as she gets up from the table to answer the door.

"Good morning Mrs. Farrell it's good to have you back with us again," wheeling the cart passed her.

"Thank you Victor, it's very good to see you again. How is your family?"

"Quite well, thank you" he responds as he begins setting up the dining table.

"Victor," says Cynthia, "I'd like you to meet my assistant Brooke Stephenson. This is her first trip to New Orleans. Let her know what you think she should see while she is here since we have a couple of days to go exploring. Would you excuse me for a minute?"

Heading toward her room her shoulder lightly brushes Brooke's. "Uh, I'm not finished with you, this conversation is not over," kids Brooke.

"It's very nice to meet you Ms. Stephenson. I hope you are enjoying your stay in our beautiful city."

"Very much so Victor and I had a chance to get around a little yesterday. There is so much to see but I'm hoping during the next couple of days I can get to everything on my list."

"I'm sure you will. Please enjoy your stay and if I can help in any way, please let me know."

"I will. Thank you very much."

"Oh, did Victor leave already?" as Cynthia enters the room.

"Yes, but wow – look at all of this food. It didn't sound like a lot when you were ordering. Man, it looks good."

As she takes her seat, "well, don't just stare at it, let's dig in."

As Brooke begins to gobble up her food, "Brooke I am really glad to hear you had a good time yesterday. I'm going to assume you spent the entire day with Brad."

Swallowing hard, "I did Cynthia and I can't remember a time when I had so much fun and good food. This is going to be the hardest place to leave next week. Brad made sure I got a chance to see all of the typical touristy things and then last night we had dinner at a place where mostly the local people go because the Creole food is so good and traditional. We saw vintage gowns, visited a Voodoo Priestess and then went to a jazz club, real traditional New Orleans jazz. He gave me a huge stack of brochures and flyers to pick through to find out what I wanted to do and see. There was so much and I don't know anything about New Orleans, so I told him he had to decide because I wouldn't know where to begin. He is so smart and so kind. I've never known anyone like him before. He treated me like I was somebody."

"That's a strange thing to say, Brooke. You are somebody."

"Oh, you know what I mean Cynthia. He made me feel very special – like I've seen the people in this hotel treat you. I know I'm somebody, but I also know that I could never afford to stay in a place like this if I was not here with you. Hotels like this treat everyone like they are royalty and that's how I felt with Brad last night. I know he was just doing his job because he promised Mr. Benedict that he would see that both of us were taken care of, but I never got the impression that he was just doing his job. Do you know what I mean Cynthia?"

"I do Brooke, and I am pleased to hear it. When he stayed to hang out with us at Café Firebird and we all had so much fun, I got a chance to understand why Jason always uses him and why he likes him so much. Jason isn't the easiest person to please, so I knew Brad had to be special."

"That's how he made me feel Cynthia. I felt very special last night. He is funny, he is kind and I can't remember a time when I laughed so much or felt so comfortable with someone. You know I don't date much and that's because the guys I think are really nice and would be fun to hang out with, always turn out to be real creeps before the evening starts. I'd rather be by myself or hang with a few girlfriends than deal with what passes for a good guy these days. Even though it was only one day, I can truly say Brad is definitely one of the good guys. It would be hard for me to think he is any different when he isn't working."

"Wow that omelet was really good," says Cynthia. "I can't remember a time when I ate so much. Maybe it's because I had a great night's sleep for the first time in months. I guess there really is something to having a life outside of work and raising a family."

"Okay – that leads me right into my question. So what did you do yesterday," says Brooke with a hint of 'truth or dare' in her voice.

"Well it started out as planned. I settled into that Queen Anne chair over there then the phone rang. I almost didn't answer it but then I thought it might be Joyce telling me she left something behind."

"Interesting," says a very determined Brooke.

"No, nothing interesting, it was just Rusty, calling to say….."

"What!" calls out Brooke, interrupting her in mid-sentence, "your mystery man Rusty? No kidding?"

"No kidding," replies Cynthia.

"What was that all about? What did he want?"

"He called to apologize to me."

"Apologize to you for what?" quizzes Brooke.

"Nothing important he just felt he should apologize for joining us at Café Firebird," responds Cynthia and having a hard time looking Brooke in the face as she hears herself say those words knowing there was no truth to them.

"I don't understand," says Brook "everybody had a fabulous time so why did he feel he had to apologize for hanging out with us?"

Lowering her head remembering how she felt when he took hold of her hand and squeezed it, she did not want Brooke to read in her expression that she was not being honest with her. "I really don't know why he felt the need to apologize. But I told him it was totally unnecessary. We all welcomed his presence and a good time was had by all."

"Something in me signals that there is more to this story than you are willing to tell me," says Brooke. "But that's okay."

Ignoring her comment "well, I accepted his apology, although I told him there was no need to apologize. He invited me to have lunch with him. I said okay and then we did a little sight-seeing, just like you and Brad."

"Okay, if you say so," says Brooke hesitantly.

"Really Brooke, it was a pleasant day seeing things I never take the time to see when I am here. He is extremely knowledgeable about New Orleans' history so I welcomed the opportunity to learn more. Usually, when I'm here I rarely leave the hotel and mostly it is to go to Café du Monde. This time I really had a chance to see a slice of New Orleans known primarily to the locals. It was a really great day."

Again hesitantly, "Okay, if you say so, I am in no position to question. I'm just glad you took the time to do something just for you instead of staying here all day and working. However, I am sure Joyce is expecting to hear that Jean's sweater is finished. That's all she talked about in the limo on the way to the airport."

"You're kidding," says a surprised Cynthia.

"No, I'm not kidding. She talked about that more than anything else the entire time."

"What did she say?"

"Well" begins Brooke "she said she hoped you would finally take the time to finish the sweater. Told me it would be a good time for me to see New Orleans and then asked Brad if he would spend the day showing me around. I didn't mind wandering around the French Quarter myself, so I almost died when she asked Brad if he would spend time showing me the sights. It sounded as though she was trying to push me on him. But then, when we stopped for a light, he turned to me – I was in the front seat with him – smiled at me and said it would be his pleasure. At first I thought I could have choked her for asking him to do that, but when I saw the expression on his face and heard him immediately answer her, with no hesitation, I was thrilled. So, that's how we wound up spending the day together. Every time I think about yesterday, I want to call her and thank her from the bottom of my heart. You know, I only really knew Joyce from the times she called the office for you. Now, I feel as though I have found a really good friend. You are so lucky to have her in your life."

Thinking back to the conversation she and Joyce had about Rusty squeezing her hand under the table and how she felt about squeezing his back, she knew Joyce came up with the idea for Brooke to spend the day with Brad more for her and not to push Brooke and Brad together.

"Yes, she is the dearest of friends," replies Cynthia, "I'd be lost without her."

"Oh," says Brooke, startling her out of the memory of yesterday and last night. "I almost forgot to ask you."

"Ask me what?" questions Cynthia.

"Brad wanted to know what plans you have for today and Friday and Saturday."

"Gosh, I really haven't thought about it. I spoke with Jason yesterday after you left with Joyce and everything is on track for the signing Monday. He will arrive Sunday late afternoon and Dr. Hoban sometime around 7 o'clock. We pretty much have the next three days for ourselves. Do you or I guess I should say does Brad have something in mind?"

"You are real funny and I know what you are thinking? He said there were a couple of places he thought I would enjoy that are outside of the French Quarter in order to get a real taste of New Orleans. Also, he mentioned introducing me to a couple of his friends. You know, just hanging out stuff. Nothing really planned. But he said he was sure you had plans for us because you mentioned to him that we would be doing some sightseeing."

"Well, I didn't make any specific plans. I just wanted to make sure you had an opportunity to see as much as you can while we are here. Actually, once everything got pushed back to next week and we found ourselves with this time to play with, I hadn't given it much thought."

"I know" says Brooke chuckling, "you are so structured and organized. Having the schedule change like this must be driving you crazy."

"Well, I did feel like that yesterday after getting Jason's phone call, but not so much now."

"Um," says a quizzical Brooke, "I wonder why. Do you think your mystery man had anything to do with that?"

"Brooke I can't believe you said that," says Cynthia with a touch of annoyance in her voice. "How could you even think that he had anything to do with this?"

"Okay, okay," says Brooke feeling as though she has just been slapped. "I was just teasing – seriously. I'm just kidding."

"All right – then let's get back to the business at hand and figure out what we will do with this day. Do you have any suggestions?"

"Well, Brad mentioned to me about going to the 'City of the Dead'. He says everyone is buried in crypts above ground because the city is below the water line and no one gets buried in the ground like they do in New Jersey. It sounds fascinating. What do you think?"

"How funny you mentioned that. It is one of my favorite places and usually the only one I try to visit when I am in town and most of the time I don't get there. It is fascinating."

"Then come go with us," states Brooke.

"Brooke after what you just told me about your day with Brad, the last person in the world you should want to hang out with the two of you is your boss. But thank you for the invitation it's very sweet of you."

"Cynthia you have got to know by now that I don't think of you as just my boss. I have considered you a friend and more like family from practically the first day I started working with you. No one I worked for before you ever treated me like a real human being. You mean more to me than just being my boss. I hope you know that?"

"I know that Brooke. It was just my way of saying – what the heck do you want me hanging around you and Brad for. I really do appreciate the invitation, but….."

Cutting her off, "don't even think about finishing that sentence and give me one good reason, just one, why you wouldn't hang out with us today."

Staring intently at Brooke thinking, *how can I answer you truthfully? How can I share with you the feelings I have for someone I just met. How can I tell you that I would rather sit here all day waiting for him to be on the other end of the telephone; how can I explain to you that after today I may never see him again and that thought makes me sad; how can I explain all of this to you when I can't even explain it to myself.* Feeling totally at a loss for how to respond to her she is unaware that Brooke is waving her hand in front of her face.

"Earth to Cynthia -- earth to Cynthia."

"What!"

"Wow Cynthia, where did you just disappear to? It was only a simple question."

"What question?" asks Cynthia.

"Are you sure you are feeling okay?" asks a worried Brooke.

"Gosh Brooke, I'm sorry. What did you want to know....oh that's right, about spending the day with you and Brad."

"Thank goodness, I was beginning to think I was going to have to call a paramedic or something."

"Hey," trying to sound cheerful, "how long have you known me? When I can't control my day and my schedule I don't know who I am. This is all so new for me."

"Well, my advice to you is - get over it. Learn to just go with the flow. How about it – come hang out with me and Brad."

"You know what Ms. Stephenson, you're right. This is a good time to start learning how to go with the flow. Who knows, I might just learn to like it."

"Now you're talking. Remember, we are supposed to be enjoying a little fantasy time while we are here. Now is as good a time as any to start. What do you think?"

"I think that for a bossy assistant you make a lot of sense and maybe, for once, I'll see what it's like for someone else to make a few decisions for me. Who knows, I might like it so much a new Cynthia emerges and then you are going to have to live with the 'new Cynthia' you've created."

"Oh, man! I don't think I'll touch that one. I'm going to call Brad to let him know you will be joining us. What time should I tell him we'll be ready?"

"Well it's almost 10 now, tell him we'll meet him in the lobby at 11 – that is if you can get ready that fast."

"I know there is a reason I really like you" says Brooke poking fun, "but right now I'm having a hard time coming up with that reason."

"But I bet I'll be ready before you," calls out Cynthia.

"You're on," answers Brooke. "I'm going to call Brad and you can call Room Service to come clean up this mess."

"Well, listen to you Ms. Bossy! It's a good thing we're not in the office right now. I think I would be tempted to fire you."

"Then who will you have around to make sure you live like a normal person and not a machine?" questions Brooke.

"Why Ms. Stephenson, didn't you ever hear my husband say that there is nothing normal about me?"

"Well, Boss Lady, I do believe this is the perfect day and the perfect way to find out - better late than never!"

"I do believe you just said a mouthful. Go call Brad, I'll call Room Service. For some strange reason I believe this will probably be a day I won't forget for a very, long time. I'm hanging out with the hip young people. My girls will be so proud of me when I tell them. They are always telling me to get with the program of course, I'm never quite sure what program they are referring to, but I think this is what they had in mind."

"Cynthia, you know your daughters think you are terrific. They just think you push yourself too hard and want to see you have a little more fun."

"Oh I know they worry about me and since they feel close to you, I'm sure they tell you more than they would ever think of saying to me."

"Not really, they just think I'm slightly nuts and hope a little of me will rub off on you. Jean told me you were tons of fun and silly once upon a time then you became a grownup like their Dad. That he doesn't know how to have fun."

"Ouch that hurts! But I can't say I disagree with them. Arthur was born a grownup. As brilliant as he is, I'm not sure he could even define fun."

Laughing, "Please don't take what I'm about to say the wrong way, I really like Arthur, but he is w-a-y too serious for me. You should try going back to fun and acting silly for a little while. Remember we promised each other a little fantasy on this trip to see how the other half lives. Who knows boss lady, you might just learn to like it," calls back Brooke as she heads toward her room.

"Who knows assistant, you might just be right. See you in one-half hour."

"Now you're talking. I'll call Brad before I jump into the shower. I'll see you in one-half hour."

Turning from the dining room table heading toward her room the phone rings "do you want me to get that?" calls out Brooke.

"No, I'll get it. It might be Jason. You head for the shower and if it's Brad, I'll tell him that I will be joining the two of you and we will meet him in the lobby at 11:00."

"Sounds good to me," answers Brooke. "I'll be ready in twenty minutes."

"Hello."

"Hi."

"Excuse me!" answers Cynthia. "Who is this?"

"It's Rusty, Cynthia. I'm sorry I thought you might recognize my voice. Did I catch you at a bad time?"

Sounding very embarrassed, "Rusty, no, it's not a bad time. I am so sorry I didn't recognize your voice immediately. Brooke and I were just finishing a conversation as to how we are going to spend today."

"And what did you come up with," asks Rusty.

"Well, right now the only thing we've agreed on is that I will spend the day with her and Brad." Looking at her watch, "hey, wait a minute it's a little after 10, I thought you said you would be tied up in a meeting all day. I can't believe you're calling me on your break?"

"No, it's not break time. We started at 6:30 this morning anticipating a long day but things went exceptionally well, everything fell into place, contracts were signed and we wrapped up everything a little while ago and now I find myself with the rest of the day stretched in front of me with no specific plans. So, I just took a chance that I might catch you in to see what your day looks like. It sounds as though you and Brooke have everything in order."

"No not really. We're not even sure what we will do. From what I understand, it's just plain hanging out. Say," trying to keep the excitement out of her voice, "if you've finished your work for the day why don't you join us?"

Masking his disappointment that he will not have her all to himself, "I appreciate the offer but I know you and Brooke were looking forward to this time. Thanks for wanting to include me." Now sounding very disappointed, "look, you guys have a great day and hopefully I'll have a chance to say good-bye before I leave. You take care."

"No wait, don't hang up. Where are you now – can I call you back?"

"I'm waiting for the limo driver to pick me up. I should be back at the hotel between 11:15 and 11:30." Hoping the reason she asked about calling him back might just have something to do with wanting to see him again, "would you like for me to give you a call when I get back to the hotel?" he asks.

"I'd like that very much," she says without hesitation and with more enthusiasm than she should.

"Great. I will be in touch as soon as we get back to the hotel. Take care."

"Talk to you later. Bye."

As she puts the phone back in its place and knowing she should feel ashamed of the way she just acted, *all she can think about is how happy she feels right now knowing she has another opportunity to spend time with him.*

Flopping into her favorite Queen Anne chair, *"what the heck is wrong with me? Why do I want to see him again? Why do I need to see him? This is not me. This man is a stranger to me yet, there is this strong need and desire to spend time with him. Good heavens, what does it mean."* Lowering her head into her hands she is totally unaware of Brooke heading toward her.

"Cynthia, are you okay?"

Startled by her voice, "oh Brooke, I'm --- I'm, yes I'm okay" as she raises her head.

"You don't look okay to me. Are you feeling sick? That was a lot of food we ate for breakfast. Are you sure you are feeling all right? Do you want me to call the hotel doctor?"

"Brooke, I'm fine. I didn't mean to scare you."

"Well you did – a little. You're still in your robe and you're sitting here with your head in your hands. Knowing you, that's scary to me. What happened? Was it that phone call? You......

"Brooke, it's okay. Look, why don't you and Brad go and have a fabulous time."

"Is that your way of saying you are not going to hang out with us? What happened to the Cynthia I left a few minutes ago who was chanting – look at me, I'm hanging with the hip young people."

Looking up at her with a smile, "well, I guess reality set in and........

"Oh horse poop," shoots back Brooke before she can finish her sentence.

"Horse poop," laughs Cynthia, "now that does not sound like the Brooke I know."

"It's not going to work so don't even try to change the subject. Also, I promised my Mom & Dad I would try very hard to not use certain language so one of my New Year's resolutions was to stop cursing, or at least try to stop depending on the circumstance."

Pushing up from the Queen Anne chair, "Brooke it's close to 11:00 and Brad is probably in the lobby waiting for you. Please, go have a great time."

"And what will you do?"

"Well right now, I am going to get into the shower, get dressed and then let the rest of this day take care of itself."

"If that's what you want to do I won't continue to play twenty questions, but if you need anything call me, I will have my cell phone with me and I'll make sure we don't go too far."

"You are a real sweetheart Brooke. I don't know what I would ever do without you and I don't want to find out, but this is your trip too. Don't worry about me – I'm not sick, I just need to think about stuff and come up with some answers. That's the kind of thing no one else can really help with, but I promise if I need you for anything I will call. Please, just go and enjoy yourself and this day with Brad. Who knows if this type of opportunity will ever present itself again and I don't want the responsibility of knowing I may have ruined it for you."

"Okay, but Brad is going to be real disappointed when I tell him you've changed your mind. But knowing you, I'm sure you will have all of the answers you need before too long. Have a good one."

"You too, and tell Brad we'll all get together before we leave." As the door closes behind Brooke, she slumps back into the chair. With head thrown back and staring at the ceiling she begins to think, *something in my life must be very wrong for me to have feelings like this for someone I barely know. But until I can figure out why and why now, it is too big a question mark to carry around for the rest of my life.* "How will I ever look Arthur in the face again and tell him how much I love him if it is not the complete truth," addressing her question to an empty chair. "Is it possible to love two people so passionately?" "That's it," as she raises herself from the chair. "Sitting around here talking to an empty chair is not going to solve anything. It's time to explore this path and not try to determine where it leads without having all of the facts." As she heads toward her room, it's her mother's voice she hears in her head -- *live for today and let tomorrow take care of itself.*

Chapter Twenty

"What do you mean she's not going to hang out with us today," says Brad. "I thought you said she was looking forward to hanging out with the hip young people."

"Well, that's what she said so I believed it also," replies Brooke. "But just as we were getting ready to leave she changed her mind. I asked her if she was sick but she said she was fine and to tell you that she was sorry and to be sure to have a good time. Brad, I'm really beginning to worry about her. Before we leave maybe I should give her a call or go back upstairs just to be sure she's okay. Cynthia is the type of person who will tell you she's fine even if she isn't."

"Maybe she just wants some time to herself. You mentioned yesterday that she is always busy with her family or busy with work and volunteer activities....."

Cutting him off, "okay, okay," says Brooke. "I get your message."

"Brooke, she's a big girl. Just relax. From what I've seen during the last couple of days, I'm sure Cynthia can take care of herself and if she isn't feeling well and did go back to bed, I doubt if she wants to be disturbed."

"I know you're right but I can't help worrying about her."

"Good, so I will just have to do double duty today."

"I'm not sure I know what you mean by that."

Extending his arm toward her, "well let's see - now in addition to making sure you continue to enjoy our terrific city, I will have to make sure you stop worrying about Cynthia and enjoy this day."

Glancing up to look directly into his eyes and gently slipping her arm into his, "as if I wouldn't enjoy this day."

"Now that's what I want to hear. How does a visit to The City of the Dead sound to you?"

"As if I would know since I never even heard of it before, although Cynthia mentioned it's her favorite place to visit and she was looking forward to going there today."

"Okay" says Brad sounding like a happy teenager, "let's get this day started and we will make sure we have a great time for Cynthia also."

"You are on Mr. Taylor. Dead City here we come."

"Uh, that's City of the Dead."

"Yeah, right, as though the occupants know the difference."

As they turn toward the revolving front door, now both laughing so loud, they run smack into Rusty.

"Hey Rusty, sorry we almost knocked you over," says Brad. "How are you?"

"I'm great Brad. Where are the two of you headed, or maybe I should say, where's the party?"

"No party Rusty," calls out Brooke, "just a much anticipated visit to The City of the Dead."

"Well that sounds like fun," jokes Rusty.

"I am going to do my best to see that fun is the order of the day. Today, she is my captive and I'm her personal and official tour guide for the next couple of days," responds Brad laughing.

"Where's Cynthia? I was under the impression she was hanging out with you guys today? What happened?"

"We thought she was hanging with us today also," responds Brad, "but at the last minute she changed her mind. Brooke thinks she might not be feeling very well."

"I'm sorry to......

Cutting him off, "hey Rusty you can do me a huge favor," says Brooke.

"Just name it," he says enthusiastically.

"Would you mind calling Cynthia or maybe checking up on her? Just because she says she's okay that's not necessarily true and I just want to be sure. Brad thinks she just wants to have the day to herself but I need to know for sure that she isn't sick or anything like that. She was fine this morning and looking forward to going with us then at the last minute, after a phone call, she changed her mind. Do you still have my cell phone number from the other night at Café Firebird?"

"I do," he says with a broad smile.

"Great. If she sounds like she needs anything – anything at all - please call me and I'll be back here in a minute."

"Say no more Brooke, I will be more than happy to check on her for you," trying very hard to mask his excitement.

"Thank you so much. I truly appreciate it and knowing you are looking after her, I won't worry so much while Brad and I are out and about. I hope I'm not asking too much?"

"Brooke, don't worry about anything and don't worry about having to change your plans for the day. It will be my pleasure to do this for you," making sure he doesn't sound as though he's just been awarded a grand prize. "Look, you and Brad go and make this a long super fun day and I assure you, if there is anything Cynthia needs, I will take good care of her for you."

Stepping toward him and kissing him on the cheek, "thank you so much. Remember, call me if you need me and we'll be back here in a shot."

"Brad, please try to convince her she doesn't have to worry about Cynthia and be sure she sees the best this city has to offer."

Sensing there was a double meaning to his statement, "don't worry about that Rusty, I've already told Brooke there is no way I will let her return to New Jersey without seeing just about everything New Orleans has to offer. Besides, when Mr. Benedict returns, I don't want her telling him that I fell down on the job of taking care of the two of them. I enjoy my assignments with him and I want to make sure I keep them."

"Have a great day you two and remember Brooke, don't worry about Cynthia. You are leaving her in capable hands."

"Thanks again," calls out Brooke as they make their way out the door.

Crossing the lobby and dropping into one of the overstuffed chairs, *'can this really be happening? Did she cancel her plans with Brooke and Brad for me? Well, there's only one way to find out, reaching for the house phone on the desk near his chair,* "Operator, Executive Suite A please."

"Hello!"

Just the sound of her voice made him feel like a love-sick schoolboy. "Hi Cynthia, it's Rusty. I ran into Brooke and Brad and she mentioned you were not feeling well and asked me to check in on you. So here I am, checking in on you."

Smiling and heading toward her favorite chair, "leave it to Brooke."

"Are you okay? Is there anything I can do, anything you need? Brooke gave me strict instructions to take care of you today."

Laughing as she listens to him race on with barely a pause between each sentence. "Brooke exaggerates, Rusty. I'm not sick I'm just trying to adjust to time on my hands. Where are you?"

"I'm in the lobby but will head upstairs to change into something very comfortable and casual. That is, unless you need me to go to the store to pickup anything for you."

"No I don't need anything. Look, why don't you change into the casual and comfortable and stop by here for a minute. Is that okay with you?"

"Sure that's okay with me," trying to curb his enthusiasm. "How does twenty minutes sound?"

"Good. No wait, make it thirty minutes, if that works for you," remembering she is still in her robe after her shower.

"That works for me," hoping he doesn't sound too anxious and trying hard to not drop the phone. "I'll see you in thirty minutes."

"All right, I'll see you then. Bye."

"Bye."

Placing the phone on the cradle and now beginning to wonder why she asked him to stop by, she's surprised by how happy she feels knowing she has another opportunity to spend time with him. Leaping out of the chair and racing toward her room, she looks more like a sixteen year old getting ready to dress for her first date.

Chapter Twenty-One

As she runs the comb through her hair one more time, she stares at the image in the mirror not sure who she is or what she wants. *"You look like me but I'm not sure who you really are,"* placing her face so close to the mirror pockets of steam create a misty portrait of the face staring back at her. *"Yes, you do look like me but at this very moment, I don't know you. I don't think like you. I don't feel like you. Your thoughts are not my thoughts."* As she steps back from the mirror slowly shaking her head back and forth – "my stars, if I didn't know better I'd swear I was having a nervous breakdown. I expected my body to start breaking down when I turned 58, it never occurred to me my mind would go with it. I wonder if this is the way it happened to Mother."

Continuing to stare at the image in the mirror, her thoughts turn to the last days of her Mother's life. *"How could someone so full of life, so strong and smart now sit and not know who she is, where she is or what is happening to her."* With a tear slowly making its way down her cheek the image and memory of the woman who shaped her life haunts her as she remembers her unable to speak, to see, to think.

Not many people knew of Parkinson's disease and Alzheimer's during the 60's, so with each passing day the deterioration she saw in her Mother as she struggled with both, raised more questions than it answered. The hands that once so skillfully created unique garments for her children and friends now shake uncontrollably with tremors caused by Parkinson's disease. The intelligence that provided wisdom and support to friends, neighbors, even strangers, disappearing daily into some unknown place because of Alzheimer's; the daily ebbing of her eyesight that robbed her of the smiles and happy faces of all the children in the neighborhood because she made the best cookies and cakes.

The face now staring back at her in the mirror doesn't look like her but more like her Mother smiling at her. *"What Mother? What are you trying to tell to me?"* Just then the doorbell rings, jolting her back to the moment and reminding her that she told Rusty to stop by. Quickly wiping away the tears and turning to leave the image in the mirror, she smiles as she hears her Mother's voice once again – *'worry about today, tomorrow will take care of itself.'*

"Hi Cynthia, I know it's not exactly thirty minutes, so if I'm too early please let me know."

"Don't be silly," as she pushes the door wide open so he can slide passed her without being too close. "You're beginning to sound like my boss who believes women are never ready when they say they will be ready and he hasn't been on time for anything in the last 20 years."

"You're boss sounds like someone I should meet."

"Why? Don't tell me you think the same way?"

"Well, it has crossed my mind at one time or another."

"I seem to be surrounded by attorneys who think they've got all of the answers and the rest of us are just hanging around waiting to be enlightened. Is that what they teach you guys in Law School?"

"If it's okay with you, I would very much like to change the subject," says Rusty.

"Well, you know what they say - if you can't stand the heat, etc."

"Triple ouch!" he says with a huge smile.

"Please, make yourself comfortable," pointing him toward the large plush sofa. "Once again, I'd like to thank you for my trip into historic New Orleans yesterday. You've opened my eyes and mind to learning as much as I can about this city and many others I find myself in." Sitting across from him in her favorite oversized Queen Anne chair, her eyes are fixed on his Johnston & Murphy shoes. Even when casually dressed, like her Dad and Arthur it looks as though he wouldn't dream of lacing up a pair of sneakers.   Now staring at his feet and unable to control laughing out loud, "okay what's so funny?" the sound of his voice breaking into her private thoughts.

"What do you mean?" she says, doing a very poor job in trying to sound as though she doesn't know what he's referring to.

"Come on let me in on the secret, what's so funny?"

"Maybe some other time," and wanting to change the subject, "so tell me, how was your meeting?"

"Oh, no you don't," he says with a hint of sarcasm. "I recall someone telling me just a few days ago that she was not on duty therefore not required to reveal what she was in town working on."

"Okay, you win!" *How easy he is to talk with, she thinks. How nice to know he was paying attention to what I was saying when we were on the dance floor.* "Can I get you something to drink? We have a very well-stocked kitchen."

"No thanks, not right now, maybe later. By the way, Brooke mentioned she thought you were not feeling well. I must admit I almost called you back to say I wouldn't stop by because I thought I would be disturbing you. Then I remembered I promised Brooke that I would look in on you just to make sure you are okay and, if I didn't check on you, I imagined the look on her face once she found out I had not done as promised. So here I am. I get the feeling that she is the type of person you wouldn't want to have against you."

Laughing at his description of Brooke, "well, I can't say that for sure, but I never want to do anything to find out."

"That's what I thought," says Rusty. "One day you'll have to tell me how the two of you got together."

"I'll remember that. By the way, speaking of sharing information, I meant what I said about exploring the family tree. In all these years I've never met anyone else named Tate. Where is your Tate family originally from?"

"Minneapolis, Minnesota. Both my Mom and Dad grew up in areas not far from the city. After my Dad graduated law school here in New Orleans, it never occurred to them to live any place else but Minnesota. My Dad was offered a job at a prestigious law firm based in Minneapolis so there was never any question about returning to the area. Generations of Tate progeny spent their entire lives in the area. What about your Tate family?"

"Dinwiddie, Virginia. Know of anyone who crossed state lines?"

"If they did, no one ever spoke about it."

"So much for exploring the family tree," says Cynthia trying very hard to stifle a laugh.

"Well, that took all of 15 minutes," jokes Rusty, "now what should we talk about?"

As she looks at him sitting across from her she realizes that if she answered his question honestly, he would be shocked. Then again, why did he cross the dance floor to meet her? Why did he squeeze her hand? Why did he make a point of wanting to spend time with her by showing her 'his' New Orleans? Why?

"Oh" he says, breaking into her thoughts. "I almost forgot. While I was wandering around waiting for my driver, I saw this and thought of you." Reaching into his jacket pocket he pulls out a small, neatly wrapped package and reaches across the space between them to give it to her.

Reaching toward him, she carefully removes the package from his hand, making sure to not touch his fingers again. "Why thank you," completely surprised. "You shouldn't have – but I do like getting presents."

Throwing his head back in laughter, "you sounded just like my Mother when you said that."

Feeling as though she has just been stung by a bee her inclination is to throw the package at him and ask him to leave. *'My goodness,' she thinks to herself, 'the last thing in the world I want is to remind him of his Mother.* Stuttering and doing her best to not sound offended, "I don't think I'll touch that one."

Realizing that was a very wrong move, "I'm sorry, I didn't mean......

"Please," she says smiling and interrupting him, "no need to explain."

Seeing that she has made no attempt to open his package and looking for a way to redeem himself, "when everyone was at Café Firebird, I heard you and Joyce talking about your friend Barbara Brussell. While wandering around waiting for my driver, I saw her CD-'Lerner In Love' and just took a chance you may not have it so picked it up for you. I wasn't familiar with her, so also got one for myself and I am definitely hooked. In addition to that amazing voice she is very beautiful."

As she removes the wrapping, "I don't know what to say. That was extremely thoughtful of you and you're right, I don't have it. Thank you very much, I love her voice and hope you have a chance to see her perform. We've been friends for some time and she's as beautiful on the inside." *Looking across the space between them into those magnificent light brown eyes and unable to look away, her mind races wondering why he did this. Why did he think of me? As a smile creeps across her face, he smiles back.*

"What? What did I do now? Although a few minutes ago, I was under the impression that you might be throwing that CD at me. Now, I'm not so sure."

"Mr. Tate I still wouldn't be so sure. It has been said that I am unpredictable and you should never second-guess my actions. Besides that, why would I want to ruin a perfectly good CD?"

"Now you're talking," he says. "Does that mean I can stay a little longer?"

"I'll have to think about that," she says coyly. "Let me.......the sound of the phone interrupting her sentence, "excuse me."

His eyes easily follow her every move as she makes her way toward the phone. Wondering whether she realizes he can't take his eyes off of her, he tells himself he should leave now but the thought of walking away and, perhaps, never seeing her again will not let him move.

"Hello."

"Hey Cynthia, it's me. Are you okay? How are you feeling?"

"Hi Brooke, I'm fine. Please don't worry about me. Are you guys having a good time?"

"You bet we are. We went to The City of the Dead, boy what an experience. Now we're with Brad's parents, his sister and Grandmother. They are fabulous and I can't wait to tell you all about them, but I wanted to check in on you."

"Brooke everything is great and I appreciate your sending a 'nurse' to look after me."

Surprised, "nurse, what nurse … oh, you mean Rusty. Well, I hope he's taking good care of you and I am pleased to hear that he is doing what I asked him to do. Be sure to tell him I said thanks."

"He is doing just fine and I will pass along your thank you. We've just been sitting around talking. What does the rest of your day look like?"

"Well, we're getting ready for an early dinner. Brad's Mom and Grandmother are great cooks and they are so funny. They've challenged us all to a cook-off. Can you believe it? Brad cooks, so does his Dad and they've been arguing all morning who is the best cook. So now the challenge is on. I am having so much fun I wish you were here you would love these crazy people."

"Well, I'm just happy that you are having a great time. By the way, I thought you didn't cook."

"I don't, but when I told everybody I didn't know how to cook, they didn't believe me. Brad's Grandmother just took me by the hand and said, honey everybody knows how to cook, but lots of times people can't eat what they cook. But keep on cooking and with time, they'll eat it or stay hungry. She is hilarious."

"Look, don't worry about me and I can't wait to hear who comes out the winner. Enjoy yourself and if there are any leftovers bring me some, especially any dessert."

"I certainly will. Please be sure to thank Rusty for me. I know he is taking good care of you."

"I'm not sure what you mean by that but I will tell him what you said. Just keep having a good time. Bye."

"Bye and you keep feeling better."

"Brooke wanted me to be sure to tell you thank you for taking care of me," making her way back to her comfortable chair. "So – thank you."

"No thanks needed. I'm more than happy to oblige. However, from where I sit it doesn't look like you need taking care of."

"I guess that warrants a thank you, I'm not sure."

"What sights are they seeing?"

"Well, right now they have challenged each other to a cook-off. Brad, his Dad, Mom, Grandmother, sister. I guess Brooke is in it too, but she doesn't cook. I get the feeling she will definitely know how by the time this day is over."

"Speaking of cooking," he says matter-of-factly, "I'm about ready to try dinner. What about you?"

"Considering what I had for breakfast, I'm not sure I should eat anything again for at least a week. However, I've never been known to turn down a free meal – that is if you are offering?"

"Well, I wasn't exactly offering – in fact I thought you would feed me."

"I see there is nothing shy about you."

"I've been called many things but shy has never been one of them."

"In that case what and where shall we eat?" Cynthia asks.

"How about ordering in?"

"Are you sure?" she asks.

"Yes very sure!"

"Sounds good to me and since we covered the family tree in less than 15 minutes, you can share with me why you became an attorney. I must admit, being married to one and working with another has always fascinated me as to why someone picks the law as a profession over the myriad of opportunities available."

"Sounds like a plan to me and I promise I will do my best to convince you we're not all bad, if that's what you're thinking," trying to hide his enthusiasm for having a few more hours alone with her.

Chapter Twenty-Two

As he easily shares details of his life with her while the dining table is once again holding more food than any two people have a right to want, let alone eat, a curiosity emerges. *Why do I find him so fascinating? Why does my heart beat faster each time I look at him and recall how I felt in his arms when we were dancing? Why does he want to spend time with me? Why do I care so much?* As her eyes come to rest on his lips she shutters with the thought of those lips resting on hers. *Till now, things have always been easy for me. I've developed skills to know what I wanted and, when the time was right, how to get what I wanted. I've been happily married, or so I thought, for 37 years and now I'm sitting across from someone I barely know with feelings I can't explain.*

"So there you have it."

"What, oh, yes, that was interesting" she says stammering.

"For some reason I'm beginning to think you didn't hear a word I said. I warned you before I started that my life is very ordinary and borders on boring, but I guess you had to be convinced."

Totally consumed with embarrassment, "Uh, no, I…….

"If I didn't know better I would think you are at a loss for words, Mrs. Farrell."

"Of course not, I mean, no, not at all, I…….okay I'm busted," she says barely able to hold back the laughter. "It's not what you think, believe me, I didn't find it boring at all."

"If we were in a classroom right this minute and the teacher called out – test - how do you think you would do?"

"I take exception to that question," she replies with a mix of sarcasm and humor.

"Well convince me," he challenges.

"You're on and you'll be eating those words in a few minutes. Let's see, where should I start? Okay, here goes – How Russell Tate became an Attorney, as told to Cynthia Farrell."

"You are real funny," kids Rusty.

"Please don't interrupt," says Cynthia trying to sound very business-like. "Your father was an attorney and for as long as you can remember he told you that one day you would follow in his shoes. From the age of three you liked to put on his shoes and stomp around the floor, so when he said that you would follow in his shoes you took that to mean becoming an attorney like him. You were seventeen when he died and it never occurred to you not to become an attorney, as he predicted. You are an idealist, and believe that everyone who enters the profession of law should be an idealist. Your Dad was a fighter for those who needed help the most but you chose corporate, at some point admitting that your ambition to reach the top rung would lead in the opposite direction than your Dad. It didn't take you long to realize specializing in mergers and acquisitions would provide the life style you preferred and now at age 37, you're at the top of your game."

"Hey," interrupting, "I never said anything about my life style. Where did that come from and how do you know I'm 37?"

"Look at you, obviously corporate law pays better than fighting for those who can't write the big checks that will keep you in custom-made designer suits and expensive shoes, so once ambition reared its ugly head, your fate was sealed. How am I doing?" she asks, while consciously avoiding his question as to how she knew he was 37.

"Well, I would say you've gone too far, but I can't say you are off the mark?"

"Okay, then give me an A++ and we'll call it a draw."

"You drive a very hard bargain Ms. Cynthia. If I had any I would even give you a gold star."

"That's okay, just hearing you admit defeat is more than enough for me."

"I didn't hear defeat – I'm just giving you your due!"

Staring at each other as they sit on opposite sides of the room, it begins to look like a duel to determine who will draw first. With no advance warning they both start laughing.

"You have a very sick sense of humor, Cynthia."

"Thank you, I'll take that as a compliment. Now what topic shall we explore next?"

"Tell me about your husband, what type of law does he practice? Corporate?"

Shaken by his question because the entire time they have been together, not once did she think of Arthur. "No, corporate is not for Arthur. He's Chief Prosecutor for the State of New Jersey."

"Oh, a real idealist," says Rusty.

"I guess that's a good way to put it," replies Cynthia.

"What's he like?"

"Oh, I'm probably not the most objective person to ask," *now feeling extremely uncomfortable sharing information about Arthur and their life together, while sitting so close to him and wrestling with feelings that can't be explained.*

"That's understandable, but what kind of person is he, not just as an attorney."

"Oh, Arthur is a very serious no nonsense kind of person, very business oriented and extremely dedicated to his work. He's a good father, dependable, trustworthy and….."

Not letting her finish, "you make him sound like a boy scout."

Offended by his comment, "that's not a very nice thing to say. I'm sorry if that's the impression you got based solely on my description."

"Please, don't be angry, I'm sorry, I didn't mean it the way it sounded. I was just trying to imagine the type of person you would be married to."

"Why?"

"No particular reason, just curious."

"That's an odd thing to be curious about."

Feeling a strong need to change the subject, "what were your parents like?" asks Rusty. "While we were exploring the Tate side of the tree, you didn't mention them."

"That's a long story probably best saved for another day. They certainly were not like yours. I have no memory of romance being high on their list like your Mom and Dad. In fact, as I listened to you the other night at Café Firebird talking about their dancing together every chance they could, it saddened me to realize I never saw my parents dance. Not even when each of us got married. However, they were married for fifty-two years and ironically, they were both sick at the same time in the same hospital although on different floors, and died two weeks apart."

"Well, to me that sounds as though they knew the meaning of romance even if the outside world didn't see it."

"Um, I never thought about it that way. My goodness, you sound like an incurable romantic," kids Cynthia.

"Well, in my world life should be a romantic adventure. My parents created that kind of life for themselves and I felt lucky to be part of it. How long have you been married?"

Without responding to his question, realizing she was probably planning her wedding the same year he was born, so now would be a good time to change the subject "enough about me what about you? Are you married, or something?"

"No, not married and no something."

"Ever?" she asks sounding more interested than she should.

"Never," he says matter-of-factly.

"How did you manage to escape that?"

"Tons of work and hiding from my friends," chuckles Rusty.

"Why would you hide from your friends?"

"I seem to be at the top of everyone's fix up list. My sister tells me I'm suffering from commitment phobia."

"Is she right?"

"Maybe a little, but when you've been part of the kind of marriage and friendship my parents had and you want that for yourself, you become very selective about your life partner. I guess I'm just a little old-fashioned that way."

Getting up from the Queen Anne chair and hoping he doesn't sense that she feels more uncomfortable now than when he first walked through the door, "my goodness look at the time and look at all of this food we didn't eat," pointing to the dining room table. "Can you believe we've talked the afternoon away? It's almost 8:00 o'clock. Room Service will think we've high-jacked their china," as she heads toward the phone realizing her feelings for him are growing. "I better call to get this cleared. Thank you for spending your afternoon with me it was very kind of you," *sounding more like a mother and trying hard to not reveal that she really doesn't want him to leave, as the lights from the buildings across the street cast a fairy tale glow into the room surrounding them.* Placing her hand on the receiver, she is unaware that he is directly behind her until he places his hand on top of hers. Staring at his hand she knows she should pull away, but she can't bring herself to do it. Knowing she should say something, she can't find the words.

"You know what's happened, don't you Cynthia?" as he moves closer and whispers into her ear.

Wanting to say no but knowing that would be a lie, "I don't know what you mean," she says quietly.

"I believe you do. Tell me honestly that you are totally unaware of this overwhelming feeling I have for you. Tell me you can't see that I've fallen in love with you and you feel something for me."

"That's absurd," hoping her business tone sounds sincere, yet makes no effort to move her hand from under his, "we hardly know each other."

"How long do you need to know someone to know how you feel - hours, weeks, years? Time is meaningless compared to looking into someone's eyes or sharing a conversation that can, conceivably, go on forever. Time doesn't define feelings and love never makes sense -- it's what you feel. If you can honestly say feelings don't matter, then tell me I'm wrong. If your only measurement of feelings is based on a timeframe, convince me how that works then honestly tell me you don't feel something for me too?"

With her hand still placed under his, "you raise the question because you know I can't answer it," slowly removing her hand from the phone forcing his hand away. Unable to turn to face him, she feels his hands on her shoulders slowly turning her around, "and because you already know the answer," she continues.

"No Cynthia, I don't know the answer. I need you to tell me."

"Rusty this is crazy, I can't feel anything for you and I can't give you an easy answer," walking away from him and back to her favorite chair.

"Cynthia I'm not looking for an easy answer, just an honest one. I'm not saying this situation isn't difficult or complicated but I'm not willing to admit that these feelings don't exist for both of us. Look at me and tell me you feel nothing for me."

"I………..Rusty I don't know what you want me to say. My marriage is everything to me….."

Stopping her in mid-sentence, "just be honest with me and with yourself, tell me you feel absolutely nothing for me that my intuition is way off base. If you can honestly say that, I will leave now and this will never come up again. That's all I ask."

Staring intensively into his eyes she realizes that to not tell him the truth would haunt her and her relationship with Arthur forever. "You're right, I do" says Cynthia softly. "I do feel something for you - I can't explain it and part of me doesn't want to. I hardly know you, yet being here with you is all I care about right now."

Reaching for her, "Cynthia…..

Pulling away, "no, please. We are two sensible people and I'm old enough to be your -

"Stop" he says forcefully, "don't finish that sentence. It's too late to be sensible and too late to forget what we just said. It doesn't matter if we admit it or not, it's not the words. We both know something has happened and I'm not ashamed to admit it."

"I don't understand how you can say that. I've only known you for a few days."

"Cynthia, stop pretending nothing has happened."

"I'm not pretending, I….."

Not letting her finish, "right now everything in me is telling me it's not right but I know how I feel and I know I love you. When I handed you the first ball of yarn at the airport, I knew. When I sat watching you at Café Firebird - your wide smile, your funny laugh and sense of humor, your sensitivity and kindness I fell more in love with you. Holding your hand as we walked onto the dance floor, I knew. Then I slipped my arm around you and pulled you close. I loved the way you felt in my arms as we danced and holding you close, I knew I wanted to have you in my arms forever. Reaching for your hand and squeezing it at Café Du Monde was no accident – and then I felt you touch back and I saw it in your eyes. I've never felt this way about anyone and I can't explain it any more than you, but I don't want to explain it or need to explain it. I love you as deeply as any man can love a woman and I know you feel something for me. All I ask is that you stop pretending you don't. I know this situation is awkward, but if nothing else let's be honest about our feelings.

"I'm not pretending Rusty, I do feel something for you, but I can't. I committed myself to someone else years ago – that's all I've ever wanted, that's all I know. We're two sensible people and we've got to behave like such."

"I don't mean to upset you Cynthia, but I would be lying to myself and to you if I didn't tell you how I feel. These feelings didn't just start today. I felt it the first time at the airport when your fingers touched mine as you took back your ball of yarn. I felt it when I looked across the room at Café Firebird and saw you with your friends – how you toss your head back and to the side when you laugh, how you lean into a person you are having a conversation with, even people you don't know like the couple at the table next to yours. You didn't know those people, but you felt something toward them that led you to carry on a conversation with them. And you felt something every time you looked across the room and realized I was watching you."

Feeling very embarrassed hearing him admit he knew she was watching him. "It did occur to me that each time I looked in your direction, your eyes were fixed on me. I thought it was just a coincidence."

"No coincidence Cynthia, just trying to calculate how long I would stay on the other side of the room before I got up the nerve to 'crash' your party so I could get next to you."

"Well, Mr. Tate, you are obviously a superb attorney because I would have never guessed."

"Keep telling yourself that Cynthia or make a joke of it, if that makes you feel better. But you knew I was looking at you and I knew you were looking back."

"Okay, so now what?" asks Cynthia. "Maybe it's best for you to go now."

"And what would that solve?" he asks. "Sure, you can send me away but can you send your feelings away also?" as he moves toward her.

Turning her eyes away from his, "it doesn't matter what or how I feel. I'm not free to love you."

"It matters to me, Cynthia," as he gently slides his hands around her waist and pulls her gently to him. "I love you, let me love you."

"I can't, I can't, even if I wanted to give in to my feelings please understand that I can't," she whispers. Pulling away from him "I know what love feels like but no one, especially me, falls in love like this and this fast." *Remembering another time and replaying those words in her head, she thinks - that's not true. At 15 I fell in love with Arthur the minute I saw him, but that's what 15 year olds do, not someone 58. Thinking of Arthur at this moment should be enough to strangle me with feelings of guilt, but looking into his eyes the only thing I know is that I want Rusty to hold me close and to kiss me. Trying to resist thinking about what is right and what is wrong and hearing her mother's voice – 'live for today, tomorrow will take care of itself'* - she raises her arms and slowly, gently slides them around his neck pulling him closer and pressing her body into his until her mouth opens to meet his soft, moist lips. Locked in his arms with her body molded against his, she is lost in the moment of Cynthia the woman - not Cynthia the wife, Cynthia the Mom, Cynthia the executive, Cynthia the doer. For now, for this time where emotions swing back and forth and setting aside all barriers where there is no right or wrong, for this brief moment she allows herself to love him.

The shrill sound of the doorbell jolts her back to reality as she quickly removes her arms from around his neck like a six year old caught playing house. Believing its Room Service she immediately opens the door as Rusty walks back into the living room to the sofa.

"Jason!"

"Hey Cynthia" as he pushes passed her, unaware she is not alone. "Well that's some greeting, you sound totally surprised to see me."

"I am and if memory serves me correctly, I was under the impression you would not be back until Sunday. Thanks for the heads up."

Swinging around with his back to the living room, "what are you talking about? I called and left a message for you early this afternoon to let you know I would be heading back to the hotel tonight by 8:00 o'clock."

"Well I never received any message. Nothing was delivered to me."

Glancing toward the floor, he spots a familiar envelope. Pointing toward the floor, "then I guess you never saw this" reaching down to retrieve it.

"No, I guess I didn't," she says feeling slightly embarrassed.

"Don't worry about it, I guess with all the sights you and Brooke took in today, an envelope slipped under your door was not exactly high on your list. Hoban is returning from Switzerland tonight, meeting is scheduled for 10:00 a.m. tomorrow morning, all of the papers for the merger will be signed, and our work here will be done." Glancing over her shoulder, he spots the mounts of food on the dining table. Handing the envelope to her, he brushes passed her completely unaware of Rusty's presence on the other side of the room, "wow, for two very small people you and Brooke certainly have trucker's appetites, look at all of this food. If you keep this up, those size 4 shapes will disappear in a heartbeat. Can I have the leftovers?" Turning away from the table, he sees Rusty now standing next to her. Not sure what to say and sensing he may have interrupted an awkward moment he walks toward him and extends his hand, "hi there, I'm Jason Benedict."

"Hello, Russell Tate, better known as Rusty to friends and family."

"Well, it's nice to meet you Rusty."

The silence after the introductions was as uncomfortable as someone pointing out there is toilet paper stuck all over the bottom of your shoe. Trying to ease her feeling of guilt the only thing she can think to say is "glad to hear you think I'm a size 4, which I haven't been since I was 14."

"Man I'm starving" says Jason, picking up a clean plate and loading it with most of the leftovers--breaking through the climate his unannounced presence seems to have created. "Where's Brooke?"

Reaching for his very full plate and ignoring his question about Brooke, "give me that Jason I'll heat it up for you. We ate several hours ago and everything is cold."

"Thanks Cynthia, I love it when you take care of me like this."

"Very funny, just don't get use to it. I can assure you it won't happen again."

As he watches her disappear into the kitchen, he's not sure whether her comment "it won't happen again" is about heating his food or a private moment he interrupted.

Making his way to the Queen Anne chair, "so Rusty, what brings you to New Orleans or do you live here?"

"Like you and Cynthia, business. I'm an attorney." Sensing this would be a good time to leave before he is asked any more questions, "do me a favor Jason, please let Cynthia know I had to leave" as he makes his way toward the front door.

"Sure I'll do that," making no attempt to persuade him to stay and join them.

"Thanks, it was nice meeting you. Good-bye."

"Good-bye," says Jason watching the door close slowly behind him.

"I hope this is hot enough for you," handing the plate to Jason and glancing around the room. "Uh, what happened to Rusty?"

"Not sure, we shook hands, we chatted, we made nice then he left," as he removes the plate from her hand.

"Is that supposed to be funny," scolds Cynthia

"Not at all, you tell me," making his way to the dining table.

"There's nothing to tell."

"Are you sure about that?"

Moving to the other side of the room as he begins to eat, "I'm not sure of anything right now Jason."

"In some way that doesn't surprise me. Look Cynthia, you don't owe me any explanation. I…

Interrupting him, "Jason, I don't understand what's happening to me. I'm an ordinary woman, happily married and in my entire adult life never thought of my life with anyone but Arthur. What's so shameful about it is that I didn't think – no, I never knew I could feel as intensely about anyone other than Arthur. Then along comes this total stranger and I'm questioning my love for my husband."

Getting up from the table, "stop, Cynthia. First, it's none of my business. Second, having these feelings doesn't make you a bad person or love Arthur any less." Reaching to put his arms around her as she begins to cry "if this experience says anything at all, it is I'll have to make sure you never have any more days off that are not totally planned out ahead of time."

Pushing away from him, "What? What," totally at a loss for words.

Smiling "Cynthia, even I've been in love with you through all these years. Do you honestly believe my not being married is by accident or lack of opportunity? I gave up looking a long time ago because my ideal mate was out of my reach. Every woman I met I held up to you. I looked for 'my Cynthia' from the moment I met you. I look at you and know that underneath all that brain is an extremely desirable woman and I'm sure Rusty saw what I see every day. The only difference, I know you. I know your love and respect for Arthur and the life the two of you have built together. I know Arthur and as much as I know he loves you, he doesn't look at you the way I'm sure Rusty looks at you. Believe it or not, even I looked and hoped at one time. I stopped looking and hoping because I knew you would never feel about me the way you feel about Arthur. But Arthur and I share something in common when it comes to you. We are those comfortable pair of shoes you toss in the back of your closet because you can't bring yourself to throw them away. They're showing signs of wear, but you still find a place for them in that closet because you remember how you felt when you first saw them. You remember your excitement when you saw them on display, you remember how you felt when you slipped your feet into them as you walked around the store trying to decide to buy, and you remember how great you felt when people noticed them and told you how good you looked. As time passed your feelings for those shoes never stopped you from looking at a new pair or even trying on a new pair to see how they feel. You thought about buying but didn't because those new shoes may not have been the right fit or look. The longer you kept them on and walked a few steps in them, for a brief moment you were caught up in their newness and how good they made you feel. Then with one last look in the mirror, you couldn't imagine where you would wear them, if the expense was worth it or maybe, it just wasn't the right time for a new pair of shoes. So you walked away from the store without them. Now for the first time in your life, you looked at another man the same way you've looked at new shoes and you thought about buying. There is nothing wrong with that."

"But that's not me Jason. I'm not impulsive or frivolous. My life is structured and calculated, I'm not a go with the flow type of person. What is happening in my life that I would even consider a relationship with Rusty?"

"Just think about it for a moment – a new pair of shoes, especially when others notice them, makes us feel good and for a brief moment of 'wow look at her' you feel appreciated and loved. For that moment, Cynthia the person is not invisible as others gather around to take a look at your new shoes. For that moment they pay attention to you because of those shoes – specifically to you - not to a presentation you just delivered brilliantly or your adorable children - just you. People see you and let you know what they think about you and, yes it feels good. In fact it feels darn good and that feeling does not make you a bad person for wanting that kind of attention."

"So if I understand you correctly, Rusty represents those new shoes I looked at – they felt good when I tried them on, they made me feel beautiful - I truly liked that feeling, but waiting for me is a pair of shoes languishing in the back of my closet that at one time made me feel very special."

"You are an extremely desirable woman Cynthia with or without new shoes," he says with a huge grin.

Cupping his face in her hands "Jason, I never thought of you as a philosopher before but thank you dear friend, thank you very much." Jokingly – "so-o - you looked, huh – and did I have my clothes on?"

Pushing her away, "yeah I looked and, as far as the other part of your question, that will remain my secret. Now, where are the papers we need for tomorrow?"

Chapter Twenty-Three

"I don't remember these bags feeling this heavy before you left and where's Brooke," says Arthur as he places her luggage and various shopping bags into the back of their aging SUV. "Are you sure you didn't bring half of New Orleans home with you?"

"I tried my best and I convinced Brooke to stay until the end of the week," she responded while heading toward the front of the car unaware that he is now directly behind her. As she reaches for the door handle he gently places his hand on top of hers, "here, let me get that" as he swings the door open and stands beside it as though he was auditioning for the role of a chauffeur. "I am so glad you are home. I really missed you being here."

Looking into his eyes, she steps toward him, places her arms around his neck and kisses him. Letting go of the door, he wraps both arms around her waist and pulls her close. To the outside world they look like two teenagers stealing a kiss before someone's parent shows up to stop them.

"Excuse me. Sir, ma'am, excuse me." As they pull away from each other they turn to stare into the face of a very unfriendly looking police officer. "If you don't mind, please move your car, parking is not allowed in this area."

Amused by being busted "sorry officer, we were just leaving."

"Thank you" responded the officer, "also, you would probably be a lot more comfortable if you got a room."

"Thank you officer we will take that under consideration," replies Arthur.

As he helps her into the car, "geeze Arthur, what good is it being the State's Chief Prosecutor if you can't make out with a woman at the airport every now and then? See if you can't get that worked into your benefits package."

Settling into her seat she watches as he walks across the front of the car to the driver's side with, for a very brief second, thoughts of Rusty doing the same thing when they were sightseeing. As Arthur buckles up in the seat next to her she reaches out and takes his hand, "thank you my Knight in shining armor, I really missed you. It's good to be home."

Squeezing her hand, "then that makes two of us. But every news program put you into our living room with stories of the merger. You should know you look fabulous and super hot on TV."

Realizing that is the first time she has ever heard him refer to her as hot, other than the fever incident, "I think we had better point this car toward the airport exit before our not-so friendly airport cop shows up again."

"Your wish is my command Mrs. Farrell," as they make their way toward the exit.

"How was your time with the girls?"

"You may not believe this," he responds enthusiastically "but we had a ball."

"Oh no, I'm afraid to ask."

"No, it was all good. One day they decided they were going to teach me how to cook."

"Uh, is my house still standing?"

"Ok, I probably deserved that - but it was really fun. Who knows, I might just do more of it."

"Well if that's the case, you can cook dinner for me tonight."

"I didn't say I was that good, only that it was fun. It was great just hanging out with them. Now, here is the big surprise – they took me to a reggae concert at the Meadowlands."

"You are joking, right?"

"No joke. I really enjoyed it."

Laughing, "I would have paid any price to witness that. How did they manage to get you to a reggae concert?"

"Well, during the cooking sessions they told me I was too uptight and needed to loosen up a little – you know, get with the program, as they put it. Needless to say, I didn't agree with them but then they started giving me specific examples of what they see. One really got my attention."

"I'm almost afraid to ask."

"No Cynthia, for real. They made a lot of sense and it was hard for me to disagree with some of what they said. Rebecca pointed out that she sees the two of us wrapped up in our work instead of each other.

Jean asked me if I was ever a romantic and, you know what, I couldn't answer her question. Then I stepped right into it when I challenged them to come up with things I could do to loosen up. Just my luck the concert was in town this week."

"Well then, I believe the 64 thousand dollar question is - did you loosen up?"

"I think I loosened up a lot. First, I took off my jacket and tie, unbuttoned the top three buttons of my shirt and got down with the music, as the kids say."

"I don't think that was the kind of loosen up they meant, but it's a start. I am so, so sorry I missed it."

"Don't worry they are prepared to make you feel as though you were there. They took tons of pictures and are working on a major presentation for your homecoming. Please don't let on that I warned you, but I wanted to make sure you didn't have a stroke from laughing too much. I told them if I ever see those pictures on You Tube, I'll have them arrested."

As he eases the car onto Route 24 heading home, "Oh, by the way, I have a little surprise for you."

"I'm not so sure I can handle any more surprises. Just the thought of you at a reggae concert tops the surprise chart."

Reaching into the door pocket he pulls out a small neatly wrapped package. "As soon as I saw this, I had to get it for you."

"What is it?"

"Just open it."

Carefully pulling back one corner, she immediately knew what the neatly wrapped package contained. As she removes the paper she begins to cry as she thinks of Rusty handing her the same package and as she stares at her friend Barbara Brussell's beautiful face on the cover of her newest CD.

"Cynthia, what's wrong?"

Now sobbing she can't answer him.

"Cyn, talk to me. Please, what's wrong?"

Oh Art, she thinks, there's so much I want to tell you. I wish I could tell you – but you're the one person I can't tell. I know if I do, you will be terribly hurt and I would rather die than hurt you. I've always been able to talk to you but how would I ever make you understand my feelings for another man without hurting you deeply.

"We're coming to the exit for Short Hills Mall. I'm pulling into the parking lot. Cynthia, please tell me what's wrong – talk to me."

"It's nothing Art," realizing she could never tell him about Rusty and her feelings for him. "I'm just tired, I'm relieved the merger is over and I am really glad to be home."

"Are you sure? You seemed so far away. Are you really sure?" as he pulls into a spot to park.

"I'm sure Arthur, I'm really sure."

Turning to look at her and staring as though seeing her for the first time he raises his hand to wipe away the tears falling down her cheeks. "I am so in love with you and I missed you so much," as he slowly places his soft lips on hers.

Pulling away, she stares deeply into the eyes and face of the man she has known and loved for most of her life. "You know, I think our not so friendly police officer had the right idea."

"What idea?"

"Getting a room sounds pretty good to me right now."

"Mrs. Farrell, you're on. Oh – wait! We can't."

"You're kidding, right?"

"No, I'm not kidding. But believe me there is a good reason."

"Well, that reason better be better than good."

"I was told not to tell you but I guess I have no choice now."

"Not to tell me what?"

"Rebecca, Jean, Joyce and Mavis have cooked up a surprise for you. It's kind of a welcome home, we are proud of you, you rock celebration. You know, your sister Mavis is a real piece of work. All week she has been ordering everyone around like a drill sergeant and for someone approaching 80, she has more energy than the other three all put together. But please, please when we get home don't let on that you know about it," pulling out of the parking lot and heading toward the highway.

"Well, if going home is my only option right now, don't worry my darling your secret is safe with me. I'm very good at keeping secrets!"

Chapter Twenty-Four

Approaching the house a huge banner hailing her return and large enough to be seen by everyone, whether they live in or outside of the neighborhood, screams CYNTHIA TATE FARRELL --- YOU ROCK!!

"Oh my stars!"

"Now, now, be a good girl. They worked very hard on this and they love you very much. For days even my Mom has been acting as though she is in a bake-off contest."

As they pull into the driveway standing on the porch is Art's Mom in the apron she made for her four Christmas' ago together with Mavis and Will, her only remaining siblings, with their arms wrapped around Rebecca and Jean. Looking over the crowd of friends and neighbors with Joyce smack in the middle waving a flag trumpeting – Girl Power, she can no longer stop the tears from streaming down her face as thoughts of Rusty haunt her. As Art gently turns her head toward him and begins kissing away the tears, "I hope you know how special you are and how very much we all love you. I am truly proud to be your husband. Welcome home, Mrs. Farrell - a very warm welcome home."

"Hey you two," shouts a familiar voice on the other side of the still closed window, interrupting their private moment, "enough all ready - get in this house or get a room."

Glancing toward their daughters with their faces pressed against the glass, laughter fills the car thinking back to the police officer at the airport. "Shame on you—don't you know you people are too old for that kind of stuff," scolds Rebecca.

"And don't you know you're never too old," scolds Arthur as he makes his way out of the car to the passenger side. As he opens the door, Cynthia swings around to take his extended hand. "I hope you're ready for this Mrs. Farrell?"

"Mr. Farrell, I am more than ready!"

About the Author

C. Fleming Johnson is an Organizational Development/Training specialist, certified career counselor, motivational speaker and educator. Born and raised in Elizabeth, New Jersey, retired as VP of Human Resources. Currently living in North Carolina with husband Norman, she is redirecting her corporate energy toward volunteer work and writing.

LaVergne, TN USA
19 October 2009

161311LV00002B/29/P